"I'd better take you to your room,

before I go getting ideas," Nick said.

"So you *do* occasionally get less-than-proper ideas, do you?" Dawn replied with an angry toss of her head.

This was really too much, Nick thought, for her to taunt him after he'd kept himself in check all evening. "I think that idea is called 'kissing,' isn't it? I seem to remember reading about it in somebody's thesis."

"I hope the thesis was more enlightening than the history books you read. *They* don't seem to have taught you much."

"What's that supposed to mean?" he demanded.

"Just that I've had to correct your history."

He narrowed his eyes, and his heart thudded angrily. "Are you suggesting that you might correct my technique in the other field?"

"Oh, no. I'm just a rank amateur—like you."

His voice was a silken whisper. "Maybe we can learn together."

Dear Reader,

Welcome to Silhouette—experience the magic of the wonderful world where two people fall in love. Meet heroines that will make you cheer for their happiness, and heroes (be they the boy next door or a handsome, mysterious stranger) who will win your heart. Silhouette Romance reflects the magic of love—sweeping you away with books that will make you laugh and cry, heartwarming, poignant stories that will move you time and time again.

In the coming months we're publishing romances by many of your all-time favorites, such as Diana Palmer, Brittany Young, Sondra Stanford and Annette Broadrick. Your response to these authors and our other Silhouette Romance authors has served as a touchstone for us, and we're pleased to bring you more books with Silhouette's distinctive medley of charm, wit and—above all—*romance*.

I hope you enjoy this book and the many stories to come. Experience the magic!

Sincerely,

Tara Hughes
Senior Editor
Silhouette Books

JOAN SMITH

Thrill of
the Chase

Silhouette *Romance*

Published by Silhouette Books New York

America's Publisher of Contemporary Romance

JOAN SMITH

has written many Regency romances, but likes working with the greater freedom of contemporaries. She also enjoys mysteries and Gothics, collects Japanese porcelain and is a passionate gardener. A native of Canada, she is the mother of three.

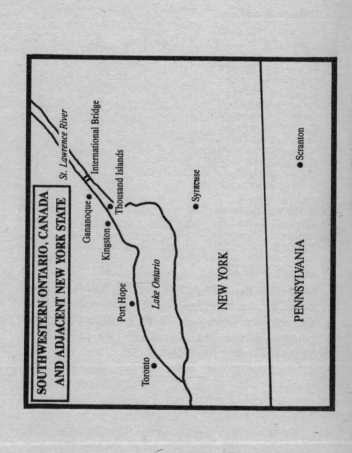

SOUTHWESTERN ONTARIO, CANADA
AND ADJACENT NEW YORK STATE

St. Lawrence River

International Bridge

Gananoque

Thousand Islands

Kingston

Syracuse

Port Hope

Lake Ontario

Toronto

NEW YORK

PENNSYLVANIA

Scranton

Books by Joan Smith

Silhouette Romance

Next Year's Blonde #234
Caprice #255
From Now On #269
Chance of a Lifetime #288
Best of Enemies #302
Trouble in Paradise #315
Future Perfect #325
Tender Takeover #343
The Yielding Art #354
The Infamous Madam X #430
Where There's a Will #452
Dear Corrie #546
If You Love Me #562
By Hook or By Crook #591
After the Storm #617
Maybe Next Time #635
It Takes Two #656
Thrill of the Chase #669

JOAN SMITH

has written many Regency romances, but likes working with the greater freedom of contemporaries. She also enjoys mysteries and Gothics, collects Japanese porcelain and is a passionate gardener. A native of Canada, she is the mother of three.

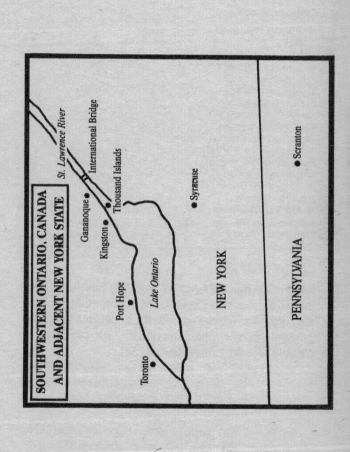

SOUTHWESTERN ONTARIO, CANADA
AND ADJACENT NEW YORK STATE

St. Lawrence River

International Bridge

Gananoque

Kingston

Thousand Islands

Port Hope

Lake Ontario

Syracuse

Toronto

NEW YORK

PENNSYLVANIA

Scranton

Chapter One

Dawn Roberts looked over the other passengers in the bus and decided she wasn't really missing anything by sitting with old Mr. Hofstetter. Her main regret was that he had the window seat. As far as she could see, there wasn't a really interesting man on the tour, anyway. Their guide wasn't bad looking, but his job wasn't to look after just one person. Gloria Barker, the lissome blonde wearing a mini that hardly covered her hips, was sitting with the only passable male, and he was just passable.

"And these," Mr. Hofstetter said, showing Dawn a brown plastic pill bottle, "are called beta blockers. They keep me from getting too excited, but they rob me of my strength."

Mr. Hofstetter seemed like a nice old man. His grizzled hair and twinkling glasses reminded Dawn of her grandfather. She had found out that Mr. Hofstetter suffered from high blood pressure and a weak heart, along with other more minor complications. He had already given her an outline of his diet and shown her his diuretic pills and his angina suppressor.

Dawn felt sorry for him, but she hadn't planned to spend her vacation with an aging and invalid stranger. This tour was the highlight of her summer. Of course a week-long bus trip to Canada wasn't exactly the grand tour, but it was all she could afford. If it hadn't been for the Pennypinchers' Travel Club, she wouldn't even be on this bus. She'd be in her backyard, or on her bicycle. With her college loan to pay off, she couldn't afford to even *think* about a car yet.

The two dozen tour members had met at Syracuse that morning to become acquainted over breakfast. Their guide, Mac Sempleton, had made sure they were all introduced to each other. Most of them were local people, but Dawn had come from Scranton, Pennsylvania, and a few of them were from even farther away. The bus had left Syracuse at ten, and for the past hundred miles, Mr. Hofstetter had been her companion. As he droned on, Dawn wondered where he was from. His name and accent sounded German, or maybe Dutch.

He put the last of his pills away and they both fell silent, looking out at the passing scenery. A herd of Holsteins grazing in a sun-dappled meadow looked as peaceful as a postcard. It had been a good idea to take this tour. She was seeing a part of her own country she hadn't seen before. Upper New York State was only a few hundred miles from her home, but she'd never been farther north than New York City. Everyone should know what their own country looked like.

It was the Canadian part of the tour, however, that had really decided her. She couldn't afford Europe this year, but Canada was a foreign country that she could afford—barely. And best of all, she was going to see two major-league baseball games in Toronto. She'd finally get to see Roger Clemens of the Boston Red Sox live. The Red Sox were playing the Toronto Blue Jays. She was looking forward to watching the Jay's Jimmy Key pitch, too. Baseball was Dawn's passion. She pitched for the Scranton Angels. Her .200 batting average was nothing to boast of, but the local sportswriter had called her curveball phenomenal.

"What did you say your line of work is?" Mr. Hofstetter asked, trying to get the conversation going again. She had already told him once.

"I work for my mother's catering business," she said. "How about you?"

"I'm retired," he replied. "I used to be an accountant, but now computers do a lot of that drudgery."

"That's interesting," she said, and knew her words sounded unconvincing. "We all like to keep track of our money," she added, for something to say.

At the front of the bus, Mac Sempleton suddenly stood up and raised his hands for silence. He was a gangly young man with a shock of blond hair and a loud voice. "We are now approaching the international Bridge to Canada. Please have your identification ready for customs. A passport is not necessary. A driver's license or social security card will be enough."

Dawn peered across Mr. Hofstetter's blue shirt to look out the window as the bus entered the bridge. Below her, the mighty St. Lawrence River flowed peacefully by, spangled with emerald-green islands. A huge steamboat was visible below, and in the distance red and white sails bobbed on the sparkling surface of the water. She regretfully turned from the beautiful sight to get her identification ready. She reached into her capacious canvas handbag bought especially for the tour. It was half purse, half small suitcase. She felt around for her wallet. Of course it had sunk right to the bottom.

She began piling the purse's contents in her lap. A zippered cosmetics bag, a little pack of tissues, the paperback mystery she was reading, a big bottle of sunscreen cream, Paba 14. She liked that brand because it wasn't as greasy as the liquids, but the milk-glass bottle made it heavy. With her pale coloring, she didn't want to ruin her vacation by getting a sunburn.

"Let me help you," Mr. Hofstetter said, and reached out to hold some of her things. "I see it's true what they say about ladies' purses." He smiled.

"Everything but the kitchen sink." She smiled back and continued rooting. Sunglasses, a package of Lifesavers, headache tablets, her address book for writing postcards, a travelers' toothbrush and tiny tube of toothpaste. "Here it is," she said at last, lifting out her well-worn wallet.

The bus drove across the border without stopping. As they approached Canadian customs, Dawn had the idea Mr. Hofstetter was nervous. He rubbed his lips with his hand. When he reached into his pocket for his wallet, she noticed his fingers were trembling, and she felt sorry for him. She thought he was a European, and at his age, he had probably lived through the Second World War. What frightening memories did officials in uniforms call up for him? What interesting stories he could have told her about his wartime experiences, if only she had thought to ask! She scorned herself for her disinterest. The bus stopped with a squeal from the diesel brakes.

"Don't worry, Mr. Hofstetter," she said consolingly. "It's just a formality."

"*Ja,*" he said, trying to smile. He really was nervous! His accent hadn't been that pronounced before. "You are from Scranton, I think you said?"

"Yes, in Pennsylvania."

"What is it called, your mother's catering business?"

"We call it the Gourmet Kitchen," she said, and chatted on to keep him distracted and ease his tension. "We deliver gourmet meals to our customers, or if they prefer, we'll go to their house and do the cooking there. Lately, we've been getting into large catered affairs, weddings, business lunches."

"Do you work from your house?"

"Not anymore." Dawn didn't think he was really interested. He was just trying not to show he was nervous. "We have a separate building downtown now, with an office in the front."

"In America there is plenty of opportunity," he said. He stared out the window. Two uniformed officers were advancing toward the bus. "Does the customs man come on board, I wonder, or do we have to get off the bus?" he asked.

"I have no idea."

Mr. Hofstetter began pushing the window open. "Do you mind? It is so close in here when we are stopped."

"Not at all." She was happy to help him. He looked pale, and the fresh air might do him good.

At the front of the bus, the driver opened the door and Mac Sempleton said something to the customs officers, then nodded to them and turned to make an announcement to the passengers. "We have to disembark. Sorry, folks. It won't take long."

Gloria Barker, the blonde in the mini dress, stood up with a weary sigh. "They're probably going to search us for drugs," she said to her companion. Dawn remembered his name was Herb something. Herb Mallen, that was it.

"They can see you're not hiding anything." He smiled as he ran an appreciative eye over her tightly fitting white dress.

"Surely this is unusual!" Mr. Hofstetter exclaimed. "I've never had to get out of my car when I crossed here. A bus should be safer. Why do they make us get out?" Perspiration beaded his brow. He drew out a handkerchief and patted it.

"Don't worry," Dawn said. "They'll probably just check out purses or pockets or something. Mac didn't mention that the luggage would be searched. We'll be out of here in minutes."

The aisles were suddenly full of passengers. The McDougalls, a married couple with two young girls, were complaining loudly. Dawn noticed Herb Mallen surreptitiously fish in his coat pocket and throw two hand-rolled cigarettes out an open window. Probably marijuana. Dawn rose and waited to help Mr. Hofstetter up from his seat.

"We nearly left this behind," he said, and handed her the bottle of sunscreen, which had gotten wedged between their seats.

"Thanks. I wouldn't want to get caught without this. I'd be like a lobster by evening."

The crowd streamed off and was led to one side, some of them grumbling, others joking about getting arrested. Dawn lost track of Mr. Hofstetter. The group was taken to a platform protected by an overhanging roof. There was an open door leading to an office, but they weren't allowed inside. People milled around, asking questions, talking.

Gloria sidled up to Dawn, her big blue eyes wide with interest. "What do you think they're looking for?" she asked nervously.

"I don't know," Dawn said. "Maybe drugs, or an illegal alien trying to get into the country."

"Did you know you can't bring fresh fruit or vegetables or plants to Canada? They're afraid of introducing pests or disease or something. They took Mrs. McDougall's bag of oranges. I think that's silly. Herb says all of Canada's citrus fruit is imported, anyway."

"Maybe it has to be inspected first," Dawn suggested.

Mrs. McDougall came over and joined them. She was a sharp-tongued woman in her late thirties, decked out in sun visor, sunglasses and Bermuda shorts. "They took my oranges," she said. "If I'd known they were going to do that, I would have passed them around the bus. I only brought them to keep the girls from eating candy. It's foolishness."

"You can buy some more in Canada," Gloria pointed out.

Herb sauntered over to add his bit. "*My* nose is clean," he said. "Let 'em search our luggage if they like."

"Lord, I hope they don't make us wait for that." Mrs. McDougall scowled.

There was no luggage search. In fact, no one was searched at all. One customs officer handled the whole group. It took him about fifteen minutes to ask them routine questions such as where they were born, and how long they were staying in Canada. He asked some of them for identification, but not Dawn. When he had spoken to everyone, he waved his hand and let them get back on the bus.

As Dawn went to the door, Mac tugged at her arm. "Mr. Hofstetter won't be continuing with the tour," he said. "I'll make the announcement after we're rolling again. I just mentioned it to you first, since you were sitting with him. They're taking his luggage off now."

"Oh dear! Did he have an attack?"

Mac looked surprised. "What makes you think that?"

"I was worried about him. He was so nervous, and he's not very well, you know."

"People like that really shouldn't travel, but he's going to be okay. It wasn't a heart attack or anything. He was just feeling shaken, and decided not to continue the tour. He's going home."

"That's too bad."

"Yeah."

Dawn got on the bus and worked her way down the aisle to her seat. She felt sorry for poor Mr. Hofstetter, and wondered if she could have done more to calm his fears. She was sure it was just nervous anxiety over the customs stop that had brought on his attack. He had been speaking distractedly before they got off so she wouldn't know how frightened he was. When she got to her seat, she was surprised to see she had a new companion. Fiona McDougall, the youngest member of the tour, sat by the window, tugging at her red pigtails.

"I get the window seat," she said, challenging Dawn with a bold stare. "I haven't seen a *thing* so far. I'm going to write a report on this trip when I go back to school."

"Enjoy," Dawn said and resumed her aisle seat. Bested by a ten-year-old kid!

The other spaces filled up and the bus pulled out. Mac announced that it was only a few miles to their first stop, Gananoque, a small tourist town on the St. Lawrence. They would be there for lunch, take a boat tour of the Thousand Islands in the afternoon and stay overnight at Rockwood Manor. The hotel had a pool, and after dinner that evening, there would be dancing in the ballroom. The next morning, they would travel west to historic Kingston for a tour of old Fort Henry and the museum, and then they would be allowed two hours of free time before dinner.

The scenery on the Canadian side wasn't very different from the American. In this rural area, the highway wound through gentle sweeps of green fields dotted with old farms, silos and some more modern country houses. The river sparkled tantalizingly, sometimes just a few yards away, sometimes disappearing altogether. Both countries could boast of ragged, towering pines that looked black against the blue sky. After a few miles, they came to a strip of tourist motels. The main evidence that they had entered a foreign country was that the road signs were in kilometers now, not miles. The license plates were often American though, in this border area.

The bus turned off the highway and continued on. Another turn, and a sign announced they were entering Gananoque. Mac told them that the small town shrank to insignificance in winter, but in summer it wore the busy, bustling air of a tourist resort. The streets were alive with pedestrians wearing the caps, sunglasses and shorts that seemed to be de rigueur for travelers. Fiona seemed interested in some commercial house of horrors, and Dawn thought of her mother when she saw some antique stores.

The bus drove through town, and at the western edge it pulled in at an elegant old stone mansion on the water. The neon sign in front looked anachronistic. It said Rockwood Manor; Rooms, Meals, Pool. The pool would be welcome!

The passengers rose and began filing out. While Dawn was waiting for her luggage, she examined the hotel. It was three stories high, with every window gleaming in the sun. It had obviously begun life as a private residence, probably the summer home of some wealthy family. The beautifully proportioned doorway now bore a discreet brass plaque announcing the hotel's name. A hedge of clipped yews defined what had once been the front lawn. A part of the lawn had been used for a driveway, leading to a parking lot for guests on the east side.

Mac called out, and the group clustered around to hear his announcement. "You'll be given your room numbers at the front desk. At thirteen hundred hours we meet for lunch on the patio in the rear. Please try not to be late, folks."

"What does he mean, thirteen hundred hours?" Fiona asked her mother.

"One o'clock, dear. Now come along. Traveling is so broadening for the children," Mrs. McDougall said to her husband.

Dawn had paid the extra money to have a private room and bath. It was a small suite, but prettily done up with rose-sprigged wallpaper and white poplin curtains. The bed was three-quarters-size, with an intricate brass headboard and a woven white spread. Best of all, her bedroom had a view of the river. She looked down on the patio, where tables were laid for their luncheon. She didn't bother unpacking as it was already a quarter to one. She just hung up the two good dresses she'd brought with her and went to freshen up.

The woman in the mirror looked frazzled from the bus trip. Dawn wore her strawberry-blond hair short, as it was too unruly to keep long. Between the heat and the humidity, the curls had tightened till they looked like a cap. She brushed them out noticing how the lamplight turned them to orange. She had a strong aversion to red hair, and she called herself a strawberry-blonde, to avoid the word.

Like many redheads, she was light complexioned. The sun was murder on her skin. Her nose already held a sprinkling of freckles. She got her sunscreen from her big purse and spread it evenly over her face, then her arms and hands. This done, she applied a little green eye shadow to bring out the green of her eyes. If she had to have strawberry-blond hair, at least she was glad she had green eyes. They seemed to go together. A flick of lipstick, and she was ready to join the others for lunch.

She stood back to survey herself, and admitted regretfully that she didn't look a day over eighteen. When would she start to look like the twenty-two years she had reached? She decided it was her height, just five feet two inches, that made her look so childish. Of course the khaki Bermuda shorts and loose white T-shirt didn't help. Not that it mattered. There wasn't a really attractive man on the tour anyway, and glorious Gloria had attached herself to the only half-presentable one. Dawn put her sunscreen back into her purse, thinking she might want to reapply it during the boat tour, then slung the bag over her shoulder and hurried downstairs.

A few of the group members had begun gathering on the patio, oohing and aahing over the stunning view. The water was dotted with pleasure craft and some young men on windsurfing boards. A cooling breeze wafted over the patio, and the lapping of the water on the rocks below sounded cool, too. Dawn looked around her, admiring the large stone pots of flowers that edged the flagged patio floor. The purple and green lace of lobelias waved gracefully amid the pink petunias and ivy. Behind the pots, a white trellis covered with climbing vines gave some privacy to the dining area and cut down the breeze.

Dawn examined the tables, and discovered that name cards were in place. The four tables, each seating six people, were covered with pink cloths, decorated with fresh flowers and laid with cutlery and glasses. She began reading the cards to find her place, and sit down, as some of the group had already done. Her spot was against the wall of the building, not the best view, but the most sheltered. She glanced at the other cards, and saw that her partners were to be Gloria and Mr. Hofstetter, along with three female schoolteachers who were traveling together. She gave a wistful shake of her head. Poor Mr. Hofstetter wouldn't be joining them. Probably Herb would take his place beside Gloria.

Dawn sat down and waited. Before long the schoolteachers joined her, lamenting Hofstetter's empty place. To Dawn it felt like a hen party, all women. It wasn't the way she had pictured her vacation, but she was determined to enjoy it anyway. She reminded herself that she didn't need a date for the ball games, and they were what she was really looking forward to.

She turned to the woman beside her and said, "I'm Dawn Roberts. I think your name is Edmonds, isn't it?"

Miss Edmonds looked the way Dawn thought a schoolteacher should look. She had brown hair just turning gray, glasses, a kind but stern expression and wore a shirtwaist dress. "That's right. Who is that with Miss Barker?" the woman asked. "I saw him in the lobby when I came down."

Dawn turned toward the door and saw Gloria peacocking in, hanging on the arm of an outrageously handsome man. "She's a fast worker, but he can't join her for dinner," Dawn added. "He's not on our tour."

They all stared shamelessly as Gloria and her new acquisition went to look out over the water. They certainly made a striking pair, Gloria tall, tan, blond and gorgeous, and the man dark and handsome. Dawn figured he must be taller than six feet, and his straight, proud posture seemed to accentuate his height. His light business suit also set him apart from the tourists in casual clothes. Its fine tailoring suggested that it hadn't come off a rack. She stared at him just as hard as the schoolteachers did, because he was the most interesting person present. His jet-black hair caught the sun and gleamed with the subdued iridescence of silk. He wore it in longish sideburns, and low enough on his neck that it met his collar.

Dawn was just admiring his clean-cut profile, silhouetted against the blue sky, when he turned and looked at her. She quickly looked away, but not before getting a glimpse of dark eyes in a weathered face, and an impression of masculine strength in his firm jaw and chin.

"I suppose he could sit at our table since Mr. Hofstetter isn't with us," Miss Edmonds said uncertainly.

Dawn assumed the same thought had occurred to Gloria, since she began walking toward them, still clinging to the man. The couple stopped at the table. "This must be us," Gloria said smilingly.

"Your seat is beside me, Gloria," Miss Edmonds said, looking questioningly at the man.

"Mr. Barnaby will be joining us," Gloria announced.

"Please call me Nick," he told them, giving an engaging smile that flickered around the table. Dawn couldn't decide whether the best word to describe that smile was boyish, wolfish or just plain charming. When his eyes settled on her during the ensuing introductions, she decided charming was the word. He held Gloria's chair, then sat beside her, across from Dawn.

Miss Edmonds said apologetically, "You do realize, Mr. Barnaby, that these tables are reserved for the Pennypinchers tour group?"

"Yes, I've spoken to Mac Templeton," he answered easily. "I met Gloria in the lobby, and she told me one of your members dropped out at the border. I've been traveling alone, and decided to take his place."

"Oh, I see," Miss Edmonds said. "Were you traveling by bus, too?"

There was something about Mr. Barnaby that didn't suggest a bus tour. A Mercedes, possibly a jet seemed more his style.

"No, I'll leave my car here and pick it up at the end of the tour," he said. "I was very happy to be allowed to join all you lovely ladies." His flashing eyes made another quick tour of the table before settling on Gloria. "It's lonesome traveling alone."

Gloria's significant glance hinted that his lonely days and nights were over. She was practically melting all over him.

"We're schoolteachers," Miss Edmonds said, gesturing toward her friends. "What do you do, Mr.—"

He held up a shapely finger and waggled it at her with one of his beguiling smiles. "Call me Nick," he said. Dawn noticed the thin gold watch peeping out beneath his sleeve, and thought it had probably cost more than her monthly salary.

"I'm Mary." Miss Edmonds blushed and repeated her question.

"I'm a teacher, too," he replied, and was aware of Gloria's look of surprise. The enchanting little redhead also looked surprised, he noticed. What had given him away—already? Was it his custom-made suit?

"What subject do you ladies teach?" he asked with a look Dawn could only describe as embarrassed. Now why, she wondered, should his perfectly respectable profession embarrass him?

"Oh, we teach all subjects," Miss Edmonds said. "Ethel and I teach fifth grade and Anne has younger children," she said, nodding at her friends. "How about you, Nick?"

"I teach—history," he said with just a slight pause before naming his subject. It was hardly noticeable, but it was there. Damn! He should have said English or chemistry. History was his worst subject!

"In high school?" Miss Edmonds prodded.

"No. College, actually, in Boston. And how about you, Gloria?" he added swiftly to change the subject before one of the real teachers hit him with a history question.

She tilted her head coyly and said, "Guess."

He used her suggestion as an excuse to admire her at his leisure. "Either an actress or a model, I'd say."

"You're right twice. I'm both," she said with a laugh, revealing a perfect set of flashing teeth. "I'm doing modeling at the moment while I study acting."

Nick shook his head. "What on earth is someone like you doing on a tour like this?"

Dawn felt the implied slight. Apparently the man felt that someone like Dawn was perfectly at home on a measly week-long economy bus tour.

Gloria tossed her blond mane over her shoulder and said, "Just relaxing between jobs. I have friends in Toronto. That's where we'll be spending most of our time."

Miss Edmonds had clearly been preparing another question, because as soon as Gloria fell silent she asked, "What college do you teach at, Nick? Harvard, is it?"

"Yes," he answered.

Dawn decided that teaching at a prestigious institution explained his expensive watch and good tailoring. Her interest in Nick grew stronger. She had taken him for a businessman, maybe a stockbroker, or one of those Wall Street types who was only interested in making money, without really adding anything to society. She admired intellectuals. Besides being well educated themselves, they were educating the next generation too.

Dawn cleared her throat rather nervously and asked, "What's your special area of interest, Nick?" A small frown pleated his brow. "I mean, do you specialize in European history, ancient, modern or what?"

She received a dazzling smile. "Oh, I see what you mean. For a moment there, I thought you had me fingered for a lecher or something, with that question about special interest."

Gloria smiled broadly, while Dawn waited for an answer.

When Nick saw the teachers were waiting for an answer, too, he ransacked his brain and said, "North American history is my field."

"That's why we're here, too," Miss Edmonds replied. "This is a very interesting area for a historian. The War of 1812 and so on."

"Exactly," he agreed, hoping he didn't look like a man grasping at a straw. And what the devil was the War of 1812? 1812—too late for the American Revolution. It must be another war between America and England. He had a vague recollection of some Americans fleeing to Canada. "Yes, I'll certainly want to have a look at the—the battle sights," he finished vaguely. Oh Lord, had it ever actually come down to a pitched battle?

"It's too bad you couldn't get to Queenston Heights," Miss Edmonds said. "But our tour doesn't go that far. You'll enjoy Fort Henry, though, in Kingston. And of course, Toronto."

"I'm certainly looking forward to Fort Henry," he said. This subject had to be closed immediately. He turned to the redhead—what was her name? Dawn— that was it. "And how about you, Dawn? Are you a teacher, too? Or are you still a student?" he added as he examined her fresh young face, with its smattering of freckles. When a leap of angry, green flame flashed in her eyes, he thought she looked more like a wild-cat.

Dawn felt the heat rise up her neck at his charge of immaturity. She had never had much to do with men like Nick Barnaby. Smooth, sophisticated, with al-ways a hint of sex lurking at the back of those dark eyes, and in his smile. "No, I work for the family business," she answered and added a few details.

The waiter hadn't come yet, and Nick said, "Shall we order a cocktail, folks? A Bloody Mary would hit the spot."

"Make mine a Bloody Caesar," Gloria replied.

The schoolteachers and Dawn declined. "I don't like drinking when I'm going to be in the sun," Miss Edmonds said.

Nick lifted his hand and beckoned a waiter. Soon after the drinks came, another waiter appeared with lunch. The subject of occupations was dropped. They ate their cold cuts and salad. Dawn was happy to see the meats were ham and chicken, and not pressed meats, which were frowned upon at the Gourmet Kitchen. Dessert was fresh raspberries and cream. During the meal, Gloria monopolized Nick Barnaby by talking to him in a lowered voice. Her tone sounded very seductive to Dawn.

When coffee was served, Miss Edmonds said to Dawn, "It's too bad Mr. Hofstetter couldn't be here. I hope he's all right."

"Mac told me he was going to be fine," Dawn said. She looked across the table, and noticed that Nick was staring at her. He lifted his coffee cup, as if in a toast, and smiled. It was a peculiarly intimate smile, and she read volumes into it. She read that he was already tired of Gloria's obvious charms and wanted to get to know her better.

Miss Edmonds set down her cup and said, "I guess it's time to get ready for the tour of the islands. Does the boat come here, or do we have to go somewhere to catch it?"

Dawn tore her eyes away from Nick. "It comes here," she said.

Gloria stood, wrapping a silk shawl around her shoulders. It was a shocking pink, shot with gold threads. "Nick and I are going to pass on the boat tour," she announced with a smug smile. "Will someone tell Mac? Shall we go, Nick?"

Nick rose, said goodbye to everyone and hurried away with Gloria.

Miss Edmonds said, "Humph! I guess we know why he was so anxious to join up with us. Good riddance is all I can say. Of course it was Gloria who went after him. I couldn't believe my eyes. She spotted him checking in, and made an excuse to go to the registration desk. She slipped a note into his pocket! Can you beat that? And the way she looked at him! I'm surprised he'd have anything to do with her. Of course she's very pretty."

Dawn was every bit as surprised as the schoolteachers. Gloria was attractive enough that she shouldn't have to run after men in such an obvious way.

"What do you think she put on the note?" one of the teachers asked Miss Edmonds.

"Her name and phone number, I imagine. I've heard the kids at school talk about it. It seems the football team get a lot of notes stuffed in their pockets."

Dawn imagined Nick Barnaby did, too.

"Are you coming, Anne?" Miss Edmonds asked. "I want to get a sweater. It'll be chilly out on the water. You should get a jacket, too, Dawn."

Dawn went upstairs with the teachers. Her interest in the island tour had dwindled when she learned Nick wasn't going to be there, which was foolish. He was a man whom Gloria had picked up. That was the only reason he was here, and it was foolish to be disappointed because he hadn't paid the least attention to Dawn. She got her jacket and ran back down to join the boat tour.

Chapter Two

The boat tour was exhilarating. The stretch of river near Gananoque was dotted with islands of all shapes and sizes. On a bright, sunny day, the view was magnificent. Dawn managed to get an aisle seat on the boat, and enjoyed the whole two hours. The guide had an amusing stream of anecdotes that added to the factual information he was giving.

She saw the shortest international bridge in the world, which was approximately one foot long, and spanned the distance between the northern most American island, and the southern most Canadian one. On Boldt Island there was a magnificent mansion built around the turn of the century and they took a quick tour of it. But Dawn's favorites were the uninhabited islands. They held a primitive aura of romance and intrigue. It seemed possible that a dinosaur might rear its head up from behind a rock, or a caveman in his fur loincloth might appear, club in hand.

After the morning in a bus and the afternoon on a boat, Dawn wanted to get some exercise. She couldn't allow herself to get out of shape. As the captain of Scranton Angels, she had to set a good example to her team. She went to her room to change as soon as the boat docked. She slipped on her peacock-blue tank suit, chosen for its ability to dry quickly and to fit into any suitcase. She threw on a terry beach jacket for the trip through the hotel, picked up her big canvas tote and headed down to the pool.

Her heart lifted in delight when she saw the shimmer of aquamarine glinting in the sun. A good swim beat jogging or aerobics hollow. The only people actually swimming, however were the McDougalls. Fiona and her sister Flora were practicing dives, while their mother treaded water, ready to rescue them if they ran into trouble. A few other guests sat at the tables around the pool, enjoying conversation and cool drinks. Dawn scanned the various groups, and when she recognized Miss Edmonds alone at a table, she went to join her.

"I wish I could swim, but I never learned," Miss Edmonds said, gazing wistfully at the enticing water.

"It's not too late. Try the shallow end," Dawn suggested.

"I don't have a bathing suit with me. It seemed a waste to buy one. I'll just have my drink and watch you."

"I'm going to have a drink myself." Dawn beckoned to the roving waiter. "An iced tea, please."

"They make it look so nice, with the fresh mint and lemon slice," Miss Edmonds said, looking at her own frosty glass. "Mind you, it doesn't taste as good as it looks. It's made from crystals. I can tell the difference."

It was true the tea didn't have the delicious tang of the homemade variety, but it was cool and refreshing. Dawn lingered over it, enjoying the unusual luxury of being idle beside a pool on a fine summer day, instead of bustling around a kitchen.

It was Miss Edmonds who first spotted Nick Barnaby. "There's Gloria's friend," she said quietly as she glanced toward the doorway.

Dawn looked with only mild interest, thinking he would be accompanied by Gloria. When she saw he was alone, her interest increased. There was no denying he was the most handsome man on the tour—the kind of man she'd imagined meeting when she was preparing for this trip. In fact, he could have served as a model to entice female travelers to join Pennypinchers.

Nick was tall and well built. His sunglasses and the towel slung over his shoulder gave him a causal air. Under his open sport shirt, Dawn saw an expanse of tanned and well-muscled chest, lightly patched with dark hair. As he moved from the doorway, she could see the rest of him—white bathing trunks and long, brown legs. His glasses gleamed like fire as they caught the rays of the sun. He stopped and looked around. Dawn assumed he was searching for Gloria. When he continued walking straight toward Miss Edmonds table, Dawn felt a rush of pleasure.

Within seconds he was there, flashing a smile. "May I join you, ladies?" he asked. His voice was deep but musical. Dawn thought it was a good voice for giving lectures, and she bet his classes were three-quarters women, all of whom took North American history just to meet him.

"Oh, certainly. Where is Gloria?" Miss Edmonds said. Dawn smiled a welcome, but didn't say anything.

He sat down and removed his sunglasses. It seemed unfair for a man to have such lustrous eyes, and such long lashes. He said, "I believe she wanted to do some shopping after her appointment. She mentioned going to an antique shop."

"Appointment?" Miss Edmonds asked. Dawn listened, wondering what appointment Gloria could have in a place she was only visiting.

"Hairdresser," he replied. "I was going to the registry office in any case, so I gave her a lift. I wanted to have a look through some old records and see if I could discover exactly who settled this area. It's sort of a hobby of mine. Many of the towns and villages near here were founded by the united Empire Loyalists—Americans who didn't want to rebel against the English." Or so the kind lady at the library had told him, when he stopped by for a quick lesson.

"Did you have any luck?" Dawn asked. She was interested to hear that Gloria was the one who had suggested the date. Really, it could hardly be called a date. Nick had just given her a lift, and had apparently not arranged to meet her later. Gloria was being too obvious, with her note and her requests for a lift. If Nick was available, why wasn't she making a more subtle play for him?

Nick used Dawn's question as an excuse to move his chair a little closer to her. She didn't think the glow in his eyes was caused entirely by historical lore. "It was partly settled by the Loyalists," he explained, "along with the Irish, who left home because of the potato famine.''

Miss Edmonds gave him a frowning look. ''The potato famine wasn't till the middle of the nineteenth century, though,'' she said. ''The Loyalists would have arrived in the 1770s.''

Damn! He should have remembered that! ''The Irish came later, of course,'' he agreed. Change the subject, quick! His next question was directed to both women, but he looked at Dawn when he asked it. ''How was the boat trip?''

''It was fascinating. It's too bad you had to miss it.'' She gave a few details about the various islands.

''Would you like to take a walk along the shore?'' he suggested. ''It's a little rocky, but I see the hotel has put a staircase into the cliff.''

The question came as an unpleasant surprise. She and Miss Edmonds were enjoying a drink together. Nick had invited himself to join them, and it was rude of him to suggest leaving. He hadn't included the older woman in his invitation, though her age would probably keep her from walking on the rocks. Still, Dawn expected more politeness from a professor.

''I'm having a drink with my friend,'' she answered coolly. ''But don't let us stop you from going, Nick.''

So Miss Dawn Roberts had some manners, did she? That was a pleasant discovery. And she had a temper, too. There was a hint of reproach in that pouty little mouth. He turned a smooth and practiced smile on Miss Edmonds. ''Would the walk be too much for you, Mary? You look so young. Won't you let me buy you both a drink, to make up for my gaffe?''

Dawn saw that Miss Edmonds was taken in by his flattery. "Well, perhaps a Tom Collins would be nice before dinner. I'll make sure I keep in the shade," she said, flushed with pleasure.

"And you, Dawn? Can I tempt you?" he asked.

"I've hardly started my tea, thanks," she said. Her fit of pique was not mollified by his quick recovery. In fact, she decided he was a smooth-talking jerk. That "tempt you" sounded highly ambiguous, too. She consciously damped down her latent interest, unwilling to recognize it.

Nick didn't wait for service, but went to the bar set up on the edge of the balcony and returned with Mary's drink and a beer for himself. He leaned back with a satisfied sigh and said, "It's too bad Mr. Hofstetter can't be here to enjoy this. I hope he's recovered."

"Mac said he was going to be all right," Dawn said.

"I hardly had a word with him," Miss Edmonds remarked. "You were the one sitting with him, Dawn."

"Did you know him before? Was he a friend?" Nick asked her.

"No, I only met him at Syracuse this morning. He told me he was ill. He talked quite a bit about his condition, and even showed me all his medicines. I think it was the stop at customs that brought on the attack." Nick nodded, apparently genuinely interested, which surprised her. She continued, "He had angina, you know. I was wondering if going through the checkpoint brought back some bad memories of the war in Germany."

Nick gave a look—a not quite surprised one. Maybe pleased was more like it, Dawn thought.

"Did he say he was German?" he asked.

"He didn't actually say so, but he had an accent, and the name sounded German. I guess it could be Dutch. He seemed awfully nervous when Mac announced that we were going to have to get off the bus."

"Maybe he was smuggling something," Nick suggested.

Dawn had a passing memory of Herb Mallen tossing those hand-rolled cigarettes out the window. "No, I don't think *he* was," she said.

Nick's pulse raced at the way she said it. She didn't think *he* was. What did the little redhead know? He'd already discovered she was observant, and if he questioned her too sharply, she'd notice that, too. He spoke in a casual voice. "Do you think someone else was?"

Dawn hadn't intended to pass her suspicions along, and she became a little flustered over what had slipped out. "No, why should I? Except for Mrs. McDougall's oranges, of course," she added.

"What about Mrs. McDougall's oranges?" he asked.

Dawn explained that minor episode. "I wouldn't think anybody would try to smuggle dope across the border in oranges," she finished.

Nick look perplexed. "Dope?"

"When people talk about smuggling, it's usually dope they mean, isn't it?"

"Oh, yes. I see what you mean."

But he had sounded surprised when she mentioned dope. "Why, what did you think Mr. Hofstetter might be smuggling across?" she asked.

He gave a hearty laugh. "Good heavens, I didn't think he was smuggling anything. I don't want to tarnish the poor man's reputation. It's just that you said he seemed nervous about customs, that's all."

"Maybe his papers weren't in order," Miss Edmonds suggested.

They talked a little more while they sipped their drinks. Dawn finished hers first, and when the McDougalls left the water she said, "I'm going to have my dip now, while the pool is free." She couldn't decide whether she was relieved or disappointed when Nick stayed behind with Miss Edmonds. But in spite of her low opinion of him, she hoped he'd still be there when she came back.

Miss Edmonds began gathering up her belongings. "Thanks for the drink, Nick. It was lovely. I was planning to go to my room and have a shower before dinner, but I don't like to leave Dawn's purse here unattended," she said. "Will you be here for a while?"

"I'll guard it with my life," he said, and even took the precaution of placing it on the chair beside him when Miss Edmonds left.

Nick watched Dawn till she dived into the water. She looked like a kid in that bulky shirt she had been wearing, but her close-fitting swimsuit revealed a more mature figure. He admired her slender waist and shapely legs. She was small, but there was nothing wrong with her proportions. And since she wasn't as young as he'd thought, he'd have to tread carefully. It wouldn't do to have a clever woman asking questions.

When he felt sure that she was intent on swimming, his left hand surreptitiously slid into her purse and began to move around, feeling for anything that might be concealing the contraband. He opened her wallet and glanced in. Nothing there but money and credit cards and ID. She really was Dawn Roberts from Scranton. It wasn't likely she was working with Hofstetter, but the old man had ditched the stuff somewhere between the time he got on the bus and the time he was hauled off at customs and taken into custody. The items weren't on his body, they weren't in his luggage, and Nick had searched the bus himself that afternoon. Hofstetter had slipped them into someone's purse or pocket, and the likeliest carrier was the woman he'd been sitting next to—Dawn Roberts.

Nick continued rummaging in her purse. It was amazing how much junk women carried with them. He deftly slid open the zipper on her cosmetics bag and felt around inside: brush, lipstick, mirror, a few cosmetics containers. He rezipped the case and continued his explorations, while his eyes scanned the crowd. He felt the package of paper tissues, opened her bottle of headache tablets and the case holding her sunglasses. Nothing.

She hadn't been wearing a jacket, so unless what he was looking for was in the pocket of her shorts—that might be it! He'd have to strike up a friendship with Dawn. His lips lifted in an anticipatory smile. That wouldn't be too hard to take. He could see she wasn't crazy about him, but he never had much trouble with women.

Dawn forgot about Hofstetter and Nick and everything else while she swam. It was like being in a private spa, to have the whole pool to herself. The water was just the way she liked it, refreshing without being icy cold. She felt the tension of travel ease from her muscles as she stroked, the even flutter kick of her legs propelling her forward. She concentrated on the arm movements, to develop her pitching muscles.

When she finished her swim and went back to the table, she saw that Miss Edmonds had left, but Nick had stayed behind. She felt inexplicably pleased that he had. "Mary had to leave," he said, "but she appointed me to purse duty."

"Thanks, Nick. Don't let me keep you if you want to do anything."

He tilted his head to one side and studied her as she pulled off her bathing cap. Droplets of water hung suspended from her ears, like diamond earrings. The setting sun was behind her, highlighting the details of her silhouette. "Are you trying to get rid of me? And here I've been fighting off the purse snatchers on your behalf!"

She was flustered by his bantering smile. "I just thought you might have something better to do," she said.

"I can't think of anything more enjoyable than being with a beautiful woman in a place like this," he said in a warm tone.

Dawn felt self-conscious with his dark eyes assessing her nearly naked body, and picked up the towel to dry herself. "That darned cap didn't do much good. My hair's soaking wet."

She rubbed her head till her hair was tousled into spikes and curls, and Nick watched, entranced. Then she sat down, opened her purse and reached for a comb. Even with her curls slicked down flat, she looked cute.

"I'm going to let the sun dry my hair, but I'd better put on my sunscreen first," she said.

He didn't think Dawn would open the purse in front of him if it held anything she didn't want him to see. She reached for the heavy milk-glass bottle on the table. How had he missed that? It would be the perfect hiding place! He watched closely as Dawn unscrewed the lid and dipped her fingers into the cream. The bottle appeared innocent.

His thoughts became distracted as he watched her rub the cream along her arms and shoulders with sensuous strokes. In imagination, he felt the satiny smoothness of her skin against his own fingers. She had lovely, long-fingered hands, with a very small ring on her pinkie finger. It looked as if she might have had the ring since she was a child. It held a tiny seed pearl. Something stirred in him when she smoothed the cream over her chest, and up along the line of her satiny throat.

"You redheads have to be careful about the sun," he remarked.

Her eyes snapped at him. "Actually I'm a strawberry-blonde."

"I'd never have guessed you tinted your hair. It looks very natural," he said innocently.

"I don't tint it! This *is* strawberry blond," she said angrily.

He looked bewildered, but to appease her he said, "Whatever you call it, it's a lovely shade. Don't forget your face," he said, looking at her freckled nose. "Though I personally have nothing against freckles. Er—if those *are* freckles," he added, worried that he'd offended her again.

"Of course they're freckles," she said, and felt rather foolish. She saw the admiration in his look, and tried to ignore it. "I have nothing against freckles. It's the sunburn that bothers me.'' She daubed the cream carefully over her face.

"Shall I put some on your back?" he asked. That would let him get his fingers into the bottle—just in case. It was deep enough. Hofstetter could have put them in there, though it seemed like an awkward place. The jar would have been in that big purse, with the lid tightly closed. A pocket was more likely.

"No, thanks," she said quickly. This suggestion left her feeling uncertain. It seemed so intimate. Flustered, she added, "In fact, I'm going to put on my robe." He would think she was crazy, creaming herself, then covering her body, but he held the robe for her without comment. "It's a little chilly after swimming," she explained. "Aren't you going in, Nick?"

"I'd rather be with you," he said with a roguish grin, not bothering with subtlety. He wanted her to know he found her attractive. He idly picked up the cream jar. She didn't try to stop him. He unscrewed the lid and inserted one finger into the jar. He couldn't feel anything unusual, so he smoothed some cream on his hand and put the lid back on.

"Why did you bother changing into your bathing trunks?" she asked.

"I like to dress for the occasion—or undress, as the case may be," he added.

"You sure didn't dress for the occasion of traveling. You looked like a businessman when we first met you. Most people travel in casual clothes."

"That *was* my casual suit. At the office, I wear a tux," he said facetiously.

She gave him a questioning look. "The classroom, you mean."

"I have an office, too. They spoil us at Harvard. Why do I get the idea you're questioning my bona fides?"

Dawn shrugged. "I don't know. I guess the expression *bona fides* convinces me you're a professor, all right. Most people don't spout Latin."

"Damned few of us cultured folks around nowadays," he joked.

"Very true," she said, going along with his whimsical mood. "At the college where I studied household economics, I couldn't get a course in either Latin or Greek. I was so disappointed. I had to make do with studying Plato and Aristotle in English."

"And they lose so much in translation. I believe that's the stock phrase."

"I suppose you have a Ph.D.?" she asked.

"Nope."

"I thought you'd need one to teach at Harvard!"

"I'm working on mine," he said. "I'm not a full-fledged professor yet. I only teach undergrads. This trip is part of my research project."

"Hmm." She looked at the pool. "Nice work if you can get it."

Since Dawn wasn't a schoolteacher, he decided to risk discussing history. "I should have chosen the Napoleonic era, and then I could have gone to France," he said.

"Or almost anywhere else in Europe," she added. "Boney got around. Germany, Russia, Austria, Italy, Egypt."

"If Mary were here, she'd tell you Egypt isn't in Europe," he said grinning.

"You know what I mean." It struck her that Miss Edmonds had corrected Nick earlier. Funny that a public-school teacher would know more history than a man working on his Ph.D.

When Nick picked up his drink and continued talking, she lost her train of thought. "It's in Africa. Deserts, Aswan High Dam, pyramids, King Tut."

"You left out the best part, the Casbah," she replied, falling in with his mood.

"You're a romantic. The Casbahs were actually dens of vice. It makes you wonder just what Charles Boyer had in mind when he made that invitation to Hedy Lamarr."

"Well, you're sure no romantic, Nick."

"I have my moments," he insisted. But this wasn't one of them. He was wondering how he could get a look in the pocket of the shorts she'd worn out on the bus. Of course he could just tell her, but even if Dawn was innocent herself, she might mention his question to someone. And he didn't want that, because there was a person in this group who did have the goods. And on the off chance that the person was in league with Hofstetter, it was better to keep his knowledge to himself.

"There's still an hour before dinner. Would you like to go for a stroll?" he asked.

"Sure, now that Miss Edmonds has left, we can take that walk along the beach. Shall we go?"

This wasn't working out the way he wanted at all. "Don't you think we should change?"

Dawn walked to the edge of the patio and looked down the cliff to the water. Below were some kids swimming, others sunning themselves. "I think we're properly dressed for the occasion," she said.

Nick saw the people in bathing suits and realized he'd have to come up with something else. "Maybe you'd like to go for a little drive instead? I have my car. Of course we'd have to change. I recommend that enchanting outfit you wore this morning.''

"My enchanting khaki shorts and glamorous old T-shirt, you mean?" She laughed. "I just didn't want to get my good clothes all wrinkled on the bus. Let's walk instead. I love beachcombing.''

It might raise her suspicions if he insisted on a drive, and a drive without the shorts was of no use anyway. "Beachcombing it is,'' he agreed, and they went down the steps.

The incline was steep, and they had to cling to the railing for safety. It was a pebbly beach, but the hotel had dumped loads of sand on top for easier walking at the water's edge. It seemed natural when Nick took her hand as they strolled along. The sunlight and sparkling water and her handsome companion put Dawn in a good mood.

"Where are you from, Nick?" she asked. "Are you from Boston?"

There was no reason to lie about his origins. They wouldn't mean anything to Dawn. "My family's from New York. I grew up there.''

"Are your folks still alive?"

"Yes, and still working. They have a business.''

"What business are they in?"

It was time to depart from the truth. This was beginning to get too close for comfort. "Insurance,'' he said vaguely.

"Life insurance, or property?"

"Property—houses, cars, that sort of thing.''

Dawn had only minimal interest in or knowledge of the insurance business and let the subject drop. "It must be nice having the whole summer off,'' she said.

"It will be, when I'm fully qualified. At the moment, I'm working."

"Not very hard," she said, with a laugh. "I don't see you cracking any books."

"I'm looking into background for my thesis."

"I'm kind of vague on that period of history myself," Dawn said. "There was a war between Canada and the States, wasn't there?"

"A minor scuffle," he said. It must have been minor, or he'd remember more about it. "This day is too nice to talk about war. Let's talk about tonight instead. Are you going to the dance—I hope?"

"Of course. I intend to take in all the perks the trip offers."

He stopped walking and turned to study her. Her hair was drying, and the curls were springing up again, robbing her of her sophisticated look. The sun caught in her hair and gilded it to a golden halo, but her pretty little face, with that freckled nose, was far from angelic. A slow smile curved his lips and he said, "I know which perk I'm interested in. I plan to usurp Mr. Hofstetter's seat beside you on the bus."

"No way! This time *I* get the window seat!"

A sudden idea occurred to Nick. Dawn saw an eager question form in his eyes, a quick frown flashed across his brow. "He had the window seat!" he exclaimed. He might have thrown them out the window. Good God, he'd have to make a phone call and have the ground in that area searched with a fine-tooth comb.

"He beat me to it."

"Ungentlemanly of him. Was the window open?" he demanded.

Dawn was surprised at the pointless question. "No, it was closed. He just opened it for a breath of air when he got that weak spell at customs. Why?"

Nick realized he had been indiscreet and tried to shrug it off. "If we're going to share a seat, we've got to settle on whether the window is open or closed. I like fresh air when I travel." So Hofstetter had opened the window at customs! That was it! He'd have to get to a phone immediately. Or better, drive down himself and give the area a thorough search. It was only a few miles. He could do it before dinner if he left immediately.

"Well, if the weather's warm enough," she said.

"Speaking of warm enough, you must be chilly in that wet suit." He adopted a concerned tone. "It's time for me to let you go and change."

"It's practically dry," Dawn pointed out. She was sensitive enough to realize that Nick wanted to go back to the hotel, however. There could be any number of reasons, so she found another excuse for him. "I'll have to wash the chlorine off. Maybe I should get back."

Nick set a fast pace along the beach. When they reached the steps, he took them two at a time and rushed into the hotel. Dawn wondered if he had arranged to meet Gloria for a drink before dinner. Just before they parted, Nick said, "Don't forget; you're saving me a dance tonight."

"I won't forget."

Hmm, Dawn thought. That didn't sound as if he was very interested in Gloria!

By the time Dawn got to her room it was after six. She took a shower and washed her hair. As the tour involved a few days and nights in Toronto, she had brought some dresses along. She chose her favorite, a cool, mint green made of fine cotton, with a low bodice and short sleeves. The skirt flared out in a ripple around her knees. Her big ivory earrings lent a touch of evening glamour.

The group was meeting for cocktails before dinner, and Dawn felt a shiver of excitement as she hastened downstairs, her skirt swishing around her. She noticed that all the group had put on festive clothing for this first party. Even the McDougall children, happily drinking fruit juice, wore dresses. Dawn scanned the crowd for Nick. He hadn't come down yet, so she mixed with the others, keeping an eye on the doorway for his arrival.

Gloria was there, back with Herb Mallen now. Her trip to the hairdresser had resulted in a new style. Her long blond hair was drawn into a French braid. Dawn didn't think it was an improvement, but Gloria's dress was very dramatic. It was a black sheath with enormous white flowers that looked as if it had been sprayed on. Herb seemed impressed.

Dawn took a glass of white wine and chatted to the schoolteachers, still watching the door. The party lasted half an hour, and at the end of that time, Nick still hadn't arrived. What could have happened to him? "I wonder where Nick is," she remarked to Miss Edmonds.

"I guess he didn't get back yet."

"Back? Where did he go?"

"I have no idea. I saw him leap into that little black sports car of his, and drive out of here like a bat out of hell." She put her fingers to her lips and smiled apologetically. "If you'll pardon my French. And in his bathing trunks! Isn't that odd? He had a shirt over them, but still I don't think he could have been called home for a death in the family or something like that. He would have changed and packed in that case. Maybe he got a toothache," she said with a frown.

"How strange!"

Miss Edmonds gave her a knowing look. "I always thought there was something a little strange about Nick Barnaby. Joining our group so suddenly like that. A Pennypinchers' bus tour hardly seems his style. Especially since he has a car with him. I thought Gloria was the attraction, but that doesn't seem to be it. I wouldn't get too close to him if I were you, Dawn. You never know about strangers."

As she listened, Dawn was inclined to agree with Miss Edmonds. There was something a little odd about Nick Barnaby. There was his lack of knowledge about the history that was supposed to be his area of expertise. His sudden decision to leave the beach. His odd questions about Mr. Hofstetter, a kind of insistence that he had been smuggling. Good gracious, was Nick a smuggler? Or he could be a policeman.

Suddenly the group was heading for the dining room, and Dawn went along with them, with just one last look to make sure Nick hadn't arrived. The meal was delicious, more like a banquet than a buffet. Dawn was an expert on food, and she knew the shrimps were fresh, not frozen. The meat was all good, "grained" meat, as her mother called it, with no pressed stuff. Even the potato salad was delicious, with a tangy aftertaste that suggested hot English mustard. But she knew her enjoyment would have been greater if Nick had been there.

When they left the table, he still hadn't arrived, and she went upstairs to make some last-minute improvements before the dance began.

Chapter Three

Nick Barnaby was in Dawn's mind as she went to her room, but it was still a surprise to see him standing right there at her door when she turned the corner. He had his hand raised, as though he had been knocking. He was looking for her! All Miss Edmonds's advice and her own doubts scattered like dry leaves in a wind. Her only emotion was happy surprise. She noticed that Nick had changed back into his light suit, or another one like it.

"Dawn, so that's why you aren't answering your door." He smiled, and walked down the hall to meet her. Nick uttered a silent prayer of thanks that she hadn't caught him trying to break in, instead of innocently tapping. Of course he had planned to knock first, just to make sure she wasn't there.

"Nick, you missed dinner," she said. "Everyone was wondering what happened to you. I hope it wasn't bad news."

A quick frown flickered across his face. Bad news? What was she talking about.

"Miss Edmonds said you went tearing out of here without even getting dressed," Dawn added.

"Oh, that." He smiled in relief. "I left something behind at the registry office—my wallet. I wouldn't want to get caught without it."

"Did you find it all right?"

"Yes." Uh-oh! That wasn't going to explain an absence of nearly two hours. "Finally. The place was closed, but I found out who works there, and in a small town like this Miss Bird was kind enough to come down and open the door for me. I knew I'd missed dinner, so I stopped for a hamburger before I came back here."

"That's too bad," Dawn said. "You missed a great dinner, but I'm glad you got your wallet back."

"And I'm glad I got back in time for our dance. Shall we go downstairs?"

"I was just going to freshen my lipstick and brush my hair."

If he could get into her room, this could be his chance to look in her pockets, because nothing had turned up at the customs area. He'd searched every square inch of ground where the bus had pulled in, and all he'd found was a couple of reefers. He'd even taken Mrs. McDougall's oranges out of the garbage and cut them apart. "Do you mind if I wait in your room for you?" he asked.

Dawn hesitated a moment. She wasn't sure she wanted to invite a man into her hotel room. Nick seemed all right, but she'd only known him a few hours. She was afraid of sounding prudish, however, so she said, "I'll meet you downstairs in a few minutes. Okay?"

Nick didn't want to make an issue of it. "Fine. I'll be waiting—impatiently." He smiled and walked away.

Dawn was flattered that Nick had come, looking for her. His explanation for missing dinner sounded perfectly logical. She didn't give it a second thought as she hastily brushed her teeth and fixed her hair. In five minutes, she was hurrying downstairs. She thought Nick might be waiting for her at the bottom, but as he wasn't there, she went into the dance hall.

The music had already begun. Besides the tour members, there were quite a few local people and other travelers at the dance as well. A small combo at the far end of the room provided music. In the dim light, Dawn didn't spot Nick immediately. She looked around, admiring the decorations. The long space had been decorated with huge artificial flowers that suggested the tropics. Some ornamental straw fans and baskets hung from the walls, and at the edges of the room where drinks were being served were rattan chairs and tables.

Dawn soon spotted Nick talking to the tour guide, Mac Sempleton. She had a moment to observe him unseen, and spent it admiring his rugged profile. The peacock chair he sat in reminded her of a throne, and it seemed the right background for him. Nick was almost too good to be true. As she watched, his head slowly turned and he saw her. She knew by his expression he had stopped listening to Mac. He was too far away for her to read his eyes, but his expression softened.

He rose at once and came to meet her. First he gazed into her eyes, then he looked at his watch and said, "Was it really only five minutes? It seemed longer."

Dawn laughed lightly. "You warned me you're impatient, but this is ridiculous."

"I'm on the right tour. They really move you along," he said. "Mac was telling me we're off for Kingston bright and early tomorrow morning. That's a small city west of here."

"I know. I read all about it," she said. "But the highlight of the trip is Toronto. We're going to see two baseball games."

"Do I spy a Jays fan?" he asked taking her elbow. "Shall we stake our claim to a table before they're all snatched up?" There were still plenty of empty tables for two, and Dawn was a little disappointed when he led her back to Mac's table, where others from the tour occupied the remaining chairs. Of course "save me a dance" didn't mean he had asked to be her partner for the whole evening, and Dawn was interested in the others on the trip, too.

The men were drinking beer, and the women were trying an exotic cocktail called Pineapple Passion that came in a hollowed pineapple, complete with paper umbrella.

"What'll you have?" Nick asked her.

"Just a beer, I guess."

"Why not celebrate? That pineapple thing looks good," he suggested.

"It's delicious," one of the women told her.

Dawn didn't usually drink much, but she was on vacation and decided to live it up. "All right, I'll try one."

The woman was right. It was a delicious, frothy drink, with fruit juice and big chunks of fresh fruit on the side. It didn't taste very strong, either, but she sipped slowly. When the music started up, Nick asked her to dance.

It was a slow piece, and he folded her in his arms, not crushingly tight, but intimately. His chin just brushed the top of her head as they glided along the floor. That dance was like a dream come true. Dawn could hardly believe her trip was turning out exactly the way she had imagined. She had met a dream man—tall and handsome and very attentive—on the first day of the trip. She was dancing in a flower-decked room, with strobe lights radiating magic beams of color that seemed to move and change with the music. Anything seemed possible, when one day had brought all this.

"Last Saturday I was up to my elbows in shrimp puffs," she said dreamily. "The kitchen was about eighty degrees, and I didn't think my holidays would ever come. Now I'm here—" She stopped abruptly before she blurted out "with you."

Nick smiled at her exuberance and decided Dawn couldn't possibly have anything to do with all this sordid business. She was just a nice kid, enjoying her little vacation. "And now you're here. It's only seventy-eight degrees, and you're up to your eyeballs in Tequila Tornadoes." He grinned.

"I hate tequila! I'm having Pineapple Passion. It's lovely. I'm going to keep the umbrella for a souvenir." When Nick looked down and smiled again, he wore a different sort of expression than she'd seen before. Boyish, disturbing, intimate. He looked—happy. That was what it was. Before he'd looked just a little like a man on the make, but now he looked nicer. The word *real* popped into her mind.

"You can do better than a paper umbrella only big enough for a grasshopper," he said.

She considered his suggestion with mock seriousness. "Mine didn't come with the cute swizzle stick of a mermaid. That would have been perfect."

"I'll pinch Mac's for you," he offered.

"Thief!"

"Only of hearts," he objected, and held her a little closer.

Was it really only seventy-eight degrees in here? Dawn's temperature seemed to rise when he held her close against the strong warmth of his body. "I can't imagine what you'd want with another heart," she joked, to lessen the tension that was building. "Unless you don't have one yourself. Are you heartless, Nick?"

It would be heartless to let this nice kid fall in love with him. And from the dreamy look in her eyes, that was what was happening. He remembered her wistful remark about toiling in that hot kitchen. This chintzy little bus tour was probably the highlight of her year.

"No, I just look that way," he said.

"You don't look heartless to me, whatever Miss Ed—whatever you say," she finished in confusion.

Nick felt a jolt of alarm. "What did Miss Edmonds say?"

"Nothing," she answered in confusion.

He studied her a moment, and decided she was only embarrassed, not suspicious. "And here I went out of my way to butter her up," he said lightly. "It just goes to show you. Never trust a schoolteacher."

"Like you, you mean?" she asked.

Nick became curious. "What *did* Miss Edmonds say?" he repeated.

"Just that it was funny, your joining this kind of rinky-dink bus tour when you have a car. She blamed Gloria, but that doesn't seem to be it," Dawn said, slightly perplexed.

"She could at least credit me with good taste. If any woman was the attraction, it was you."

"You hadn't seen me yet when you joined us," Dawn pointed out.

"True, but I did say *if*. You women are vain creatures," he teased. "You always think men act because of you. I lay the blame on Adam."

The music ended, and they returned to their table. Dawn noticed that Nick hadn't really answered her question. Why *had* he joined the tour? She sipped her drink slowly. A woman at their table called Rose was already finishing her second cocktail, and was becoming rather noisy. Mac Sempleton asked Dawn to dance with him when the music resumed, and Dawn accepted. She was glad to see Nick stand up with Rose. It would keep her from drinking for a while.

"You seem to be hitting it off pretty well with Barnaby," Mac said.

Dawn sensed a little pique in his tone. Mac had already told her he was a bachelor. He wasn't a bad-looking one, either—blond, blue eyes, tall and rangy. Before Nick joined them, she had thought he might be a possible romantic interest, despite his duties.

"We just had one dance," she pointed out.

"I can't imagine what a guy like that is doing here."

"He was traveling alone. Maybe he just wanted company."

"Did he want it enough to tip me a hundred bucks to fit him in?" he asked.

"Did he do that?" Dawn was more impressed at Nick's liberal way with money than anything else.

"Yeah, for the pleasure of jiggling along in a bus, and leaving his Jag behind. And he didn't even follow anything up with Gloria. Go figure. I hope he isn't going to make trouble for me. You're not a minor, by any chance?"

Dawn was offended. "I'm twenty-two years old." Mac couldn't be more than twenty-seven or -eight himself.

"You don't look it. It seems kind of funny he's trailing so hard after you, when Gloria was all over him."

Dawn tilted her chin pugnaciously. "What's so funny about his preferring me?" she demanded.

Mac gave a sheepish smile. "Well, now that you mention it, I don't know. *I* certainly preferred you."

There was a wolfish quality in Mac's smile that made Dawn uncomfortable and she hurried back to the table as soon as the music ended. She danced with other men from the tour, and with some other tourists at the party. Nick danced with other women, too. It was quite a bit later before they were together again.

As they went to the floor, he leaned his head down and said in a conspiratorial tone, "I've got something for you."

"What?" She couldn't imagine what he could possibly have, but maybe he had left the dance hall. In fact, she had seen him go out once, but he certainly hadn't been shopping at this hour of night.

"Put it in your purse," he advised with a great air of secrecy. He didn't just hand it to her, but slipped it into her fingers surreptitiously, closed her fingers over it and squeezed them.

She looked down, opened her fingers and saw one of the pink plastic mermaids. "Thief!" She laughed.

"I'll have you know I came by it honestly. And I didn't have to drink one of those wicked Tequila Tornadoes, either. I asked the bartender for it. You don't have to thank me. It was free."

"Then why are we trying to hide it?" she asked.

"Naive creature! If the others see it, they'll all be wanting one, too, and there go the bar's profits for the night. They only make a couple of bucks per drink. These objets d'art are priceless. Actually a penny each is the price, I believe."

"Highly collectible. I'll treasure it forever," she said, and slid it into her pocket.

He gave her a wicked, laughing wink. "Treat me right, and I might be good for one of those paper flowers you've been eyeballing all night," he said out of the corner of his mouth like a gangster in an old movie.

"If you get a chance, go for the pink one," she said, mimicking his speech. "It'll match my mermaid."

"But it'll clash with your strawberry-red hair."

"That's strawberry-blond, if you please. Steal me the pink one."

"Are you trying to lead me into a life of crime, Miss Roberts?" he demanded. "It's shocking, the people you meet on these tours. I'll mention this to Miss Edmonds."

Dawn was just going to repeat her question about why he had joined the tour when they reached the floor. The combo was playing a fast number, and between the music and bumping bodies, talk was impossible. Dawn enjoyed the dance. It felt good to let herself go, and just move with the music. She and Nick weren't even touching, yet she felt vibrations between them. Her hips moved in time with the sinuous rhythm, and the underlying, insistent beat of the drums created a sexual current.

As the evening grew late, the older people left or stayed at the tables with their drinks, and the younger group took over the floor. The hypnotic music pounded on, and Dawn felt herself being caught up in the throbbing beat of the drums, the wailing of the guitars and the pulsing of the lights. Nick was there, beside her, dancing gracefully, but always just beyond her reach. She danced till she was ready to drop. When the music stopped, she realized her forehead was beaded with perspiration, and she was gasping from fatigue.

Nick put his arm around her waist to lead her away. "That was quite a workout," he said, panting. "Which sounds better, a nice cool drink, or some fresh air?"

"Both."

"Let's have our drinks on the patio," he suggested.

The breeze from the water was welcome when they stepped outside. There were half a dozen couples on the patio. After Nick and Dawn finished their drinks, Nick suggested they climb down the stairs to the beach. They walked off into the shadows. The beauty of the night was seen better away from the light. The fat white moon hovering over the water was reflected in the shifting waves. Long arms of shimmering light spread across the black water. The tall pines groaned in the breeze, and added their resinous scent to the earthy smell of grass and bushes. Flowers that were vividly colored by day had faded to white against the black outline of leaves. When Nick took her hand in his, holding it tightly, Dawn knew that before she went to her room, he would kiss her.

The descent to the beach was tricky in high heels, but it was worth it. The breeze was fresher there, and the water lapped invitingly at their feet. "I'm going to take off my sandals and walk in the surf," Dawn announced when they reached the bottom.

"What surf? This is a river, not an ocean," he pointed out.

"It has waves," she parried.

"So has your hair," he said, flicking a curl with one finger, "but that doesn't make it a surf."

"Now you're being silly. The water's wet and cool, anyway."

He steadied her while she pulled off her shoes. His touch, warm and intimate, was a foretaste of what she knew was coming. Nick carried her sandals, dangling from his fingers by the thin straps. She discovered that the water was cold, but it felt good washing over her heated feet and ankles. Nick left his shoes on and walked on the sand a few feet away from her. They moved on slowly, not talking much but enjoying the serene beauty of the night, till the beach petered out, and the limestone cliffs fell sheer to the water.

"Do we swim, or go back to the hotel?" Nick asked.

"Since we don't have our bathing suits, I guess it's back to the hotel. It's getting pretty late anyway." She thought Nick might choose this private spot to kiss her. It couldn't have been more ideal if they had ordered it tailor-made. Darkness, privacy, a romantic setting, with the moon and no sound but the gentle hissing of the water. She looked at Nick questioningly.

He studied her a moment, knowing what was in her mind. Her face was a pale ivory oval in the moonlight. Moonbeams were reflected in the depths of her eyes and silvered her inviting lips. A breeze rippled the curls from her forehead, adding a final note of enchantment. His hand rose to her arm and tightened. He felt the hot clutch of passion, and his head inclined to hers. Nick had to take himself by the scruff of the neck to keep from kissing her. Don't be a jerk, he told himself. It doesn't mean anything to you, but Dawn is a sweet, innocent kid. His lips just touched her forehead, light as a sigh. "Let's go," he said, and turned back.

Dawn felt as if she'd been snubbed. The scenery was the same on the return trip, but the mood had changed noticeably. She no longer felt like wading and she walked beside Nick instead. He even held her hand, but the feeling of intimacy was gone. She had felt closer to him when they were dancing a yard apart. What had happened? Why hadn't he taken advantage of the moment? Was there something the matter with her? She knew he wouldn't have wasted that opportunity if it had been Gloria he was with. If he didn't like her, why had he spent so much of the evening with her? It just didn't add up. There *was* something strange about Nick Barnaby.

The lights on the patio had been put out when they got back, but a few people were still lingering. In the shadows, Dawn could see two couples. One pair was embracing passionately; the other was standing with their arms around each other's waist, looking over the water. She took a quick peep to see if Nick had noticed the couples. He was looking at the man and woman who were embracing. His eyes flickered to Dawn and he smiled ruefully. "I'd better take you to your room, before I go getting ideas," he said.

"You do occasionally get ideas like that, do you?" she said with an angry toss of her head. "I thought maybe you'd been locked in your ivory tower too long." She felt his fingers bite into the flesh of her arm and she looked up, startled. Nick had lost his rueful smile. He looked angry as a hornet, with a frown creasing his brow.

Nick felt an angry rush of blood to his head. This was really too much, for her to taunt him after he'd kept himself in check all evening. "I think it's called kissing, isn't it? I seem to remember reading about it in somebody's thesis," he said snidely.

"I hope the thesis was more enlightening than the history books you read. *They* don't seem to have taught you much."

"What's that supposed to mean?" he demanded.

"Just that Miss Edmonds has had to correct your history."

His eyes narrowed and his heart thudded angrily. "Are you suggesting that you might correct my technique in the other field?" he asked.

"Oh no. I'm just a rank amateur—like you." She turned to leave, already regretting that she'd brought this wonderful evening to such a disastrous end. What on earth must Nick think of her?

When he spoke, his voice was a silken whisper, almost menacing. "Maybe we can learn together," he suggested. He pulled her into his arms and kissed her. It was more an attack than an embrace. His lips bruised hers in a kiss that caused her adrenaline to surge. Dawn didn't know whether she was more angry or surprised at the amorous assault. It was as if he was trying to prove something. Overcome by it all, she didn't respond for a moment, but she soon realized this was more of an insult than anything else. She put her hands against his shoulders and tried to push him away.

His arms tightened around her, and his lips firmed as he continued the kiss. Her frustration rose higher as she tried to disengage herself. She was in extremely good shape, her muscles were as hard as wood, but she couldn't budge him. Before long she wearied of trying, and submitted to the kiss, but fought the impulse to return it. Her hot blood resisted, even when she began feeling strange sensations stirring deep within her.

Her traitorous arms wanted to go around his neck. Her fingers edged closer to the silky hair nestling against his collar. It was an exquisite form of torture, then, just as she began to yield to him, Nick released her. It almost seemed that that was what he had been waiting for.

His face, hovering above hers, with his dark eyes shining, wore an angry grin. "'How dare you' is your line, Miss Roberts," he prompted.

Dawn drew a deep, uneven breath that sent her bosom heaving. "Consider it said," she gasped. She turned on her heel to stalk away. The sharp swing on the rough stone reminded her she wasn't wearing any shoes, but she was damned if she would go back for them.

She heard Nick's footfalls hurrying after her, but she only increased her pace. She darted across the lobby and up the stairs, feeling cheapened, angry and already more than a little sorry. A few people lingering in the lobby looked at her as if she were a madwoman. Nick caught up with her when she stopped at her door to get out her key.

"Dawn, I'm sorry, that was a stupid thing for me to do," he said.

She looked, and saw his angry frown. "Yes, wasn't it," she agreed. He handed her the shoes. With both her hands busy, she ignored them. Her agitated fingers fumbled with the key. She couldn't get the darned door open. She knew that in about ten seconds tears would spurt, to add the final humiliation to this night.

"I'm sorry," he said, still holding out the sandals.

"Forget it. You can just drop my shoes on the floor."

"I'll wait to make sure you can get in."

"I'll get in. This is my key." She pushed, and it finally fit into the keyhole. She felt a wave of relief when she heard the lock tumble. She pushed open the door and went in. Nick took a step in behind her. She turned to prevent him, barring the door with her body. She lifted an eyebrow and said in a cutting voice, "You learn fast. You can stop right there, Nick."

"Let me explain," he said.

The sandals still dangled from his fingers. Dawn didn't know whether it was that, or his earnest expression that began to soften her mood. "No explanations are necessary," she said.

"But I want to."

She took the sandals and tossed them into the room, while still blocking the door. "So explain."

"It's not that I didn't want to—kiss you, I mean. I wanted to, all night."

"I see," she said in total confusion.

"No, you don't. I refrained for your sake. You're—sweet and innocent," he said, meaning it for a compliment.

"And what are you, an old lecher?"

"No, but I am older, more experienced. I was afraid you might go imagining you were in love with me or something."

Dawn was thunderstruck by his arrogance. "Oh, I see. You were afraid I'd be so devastated by one kiss that I might never recover. That was very thoughtful of you, Nick. Thoughtful, but unnecessary. I don't think you have to worry that I'm smitten for life. I've recovered from that attack already."

Nick combed his hand through his black hair. "Dammit, that's not what I meant. You make me sound like a jerk."

"No, Nick. *You* make you sound like a jerk."

"That's what I get for trying to do the right thing. I shouldn't have let you goad me."

"I've always heard a gentleman takes the blame for his own mistakes. Good night, Nick." She closed the door softly and twisted the lock.

In the hall, Nick stood glaring at the paneled door. Women! Dammit, she all but threw herself at him, then pokered up when he stopped resisting. And now *he* was the one in the wrong. Where had he got the idea Dawn Roberts was a nice kid? She was a pain in the— But a damned cute one. A reluctant grin tugged at his lips as he turned and went to his room.

He'd have to apologize tomorrow morning and make a last effort to search her pockets before they moved on. Maybe he could offer her a drive to Kingston with him? That would give him more time.... Or was he just looking for excuses to know Dawn better?

The sane course was to sneak into her room during breakfast. That's what he'd do.

There was no smile on Dawn's face as she pulled off her dress and tossed it onto a chair. She felt humiliated. She was an idiot. She had teased Nick into that kiss, then fired up at him afterward. What had angered her so? Was it the way Nick looked at that embracing couple, as though he wished he were the one with that woman?

Did he really think she was such an innocent little dope that she'd be undone by one kiss? Mac had asked her if she was a minor. Maybe she looked sixteen or seventeen years old. She didn't see why else he should talk about "trying to do the right thing." Unless he was married! Was that it? If so, his joining this tour was even more bizarre. And he hadn't answered *that* question, either.

She determined to forget all about Nick Barnaby and get some sleep. A shower would help after that exercise on the dance floor. She felt pleasantly tired when she toweled herself dry and slid on a cool cotton nightie. The last thing she did before crawling between the welcoming sheets was to hang up her green dress. As she lifted it from the floor, the plastic mermaid fell from the pocket.

She picked it up, remembering. How could a man with a sense of humor like that be such an arrogant jerk? There must be something she had missed. She got into bed and propped the mermaid up against the lamp. He had said he'd wanted to kiss her all night. She ruefully admitted that she'd wanted it, too. Wanted it badly enough that she'd gotten him to do it. It was her fault. On that thought, she turned out the lamp and closed her eyes.

Chapter Four

Golden slivers of morning crept around the edges of the curtains, telling Dawn that it was going to be a beautiful day. Why did she have that unsettled, heavy feeling around her heart? Oh, Nick Barnaby! She shook away the troubling memory of last night's fiasco. Forget about him and think of the tour.

She had the timetable by heart and mentally reviewed the activities for the day as she lay in bed. Breakfast, eight to nine. She wondered if Nick would be there. He hadn't eaten dinner with the tour last night. Bus to Kingston leaving at nine-thirty, arriving at ten. Maybe Nick would sit beside her on the bus. It would be embarrassing after last night, but something inside her half hoped he would. And why did she keep thinking about Nick when she had decided to forget him?

She glanced at her watch. A quarter to eight. Time to get up and get dressed. Since so little of the day would be spent on the bus, she opted for her blue skirt and eyelet blouse, rather than shorts. She hoped she'd look a little older in that outfit. It was annoying to be mistaken for a kid at her age. But when she stood in front of her mirror, she knew she could still buy a student's ticket anywhere without arousing suspicion.

When she entered the dining room at five after eight, Dawn found the only other people there were the schoolteachers. She sat with them, noticing that there were still two seats at their table. Within two minutes, the other seats were filled, and Nick hadn't arrived yet. Dawn kept an eye on the doorway as she ate her poached eggs and toast. At eight-thirty, Nick came in. He looked around till he found her, and smiled, but he sat with the McDougalls. She wondered if it was the girls' noisy behavior at the table that made him order only coffee. He kept looking at Dawn, and caught her looking back a few times.

She dawdled over her eggs, and when the others went to their rooms to pack, Dawn had another cup of coffee. Almost immediately Nick picked up his cup and began walking toward her. She felt flustered, and pretended not to notice him. Suddenly he was there, and in her heart she knew she was glad.

"May I?" he asked.

She peeped up, hiding all her joy at his overture. "Oh, hi, Nick. Sure, if you want to." That sounded ungracious so she added, "It's a lovely day for our trip, isn't it?"

Nick was relieved that she hadn't kept up her attitude of last night, and quickly responded to her banal opening. "A beautiful day. The drive along the water should be marvelous," he replied.

"This time I'm going to hit the bus early, and get a window seat," she said firmly.

"I was thinking it would be nice driving in my car with the top down."

Dawn felt a jolt of surprise that felt like dismay. "Aren't you coming in the bus?"

He looked at her uncertainly. Was that regret gleaming in her green eyes? "It was just a thought. We have a couple of hours free in the afternoon. The car might come in handy for sight-seeing." He decided it was regret, and quickly forged ahead with his plan. "Of course it's not much fun driving alone." He peered at her over his coffee cup.

Dawn read an invitation in his look, and she gave him a mischievous smile. "Gee, I don't know if I'd be safe with you, Nick. A whole half hour alone."

"I'm a good driver."

"I didn't mean that. You're so irresistible and experienced, I might go falling in love. After my close call last night, I think I should leave well enough alone."

Nick shook his head ruefully. "I'm never going to hear the end of that, am I? I've said I'm sorry. I've admitted I was a jerk."

"You weren't the only one," she admitted, and felt better for getting the admission off her chest. "It was partly my fault."

"That's gentlemanly of you, sharing the blame. You're a gentleman and I'm a scholar. We ought to make a great team, don't you think? We'll bury our indiscretion and go on from here."

"All right, but in a shallow grave," she warned. "Don't be surprised if it pops up from time to time. I'm new at being a gentleman."

"You'll come with me?" he asked with flattering eagerness.

Dawn wrinkled her brow and thought about it. She was thrilled that he'd asked her and had every intention of going, but she didn't plan to jump at it. "A convertible, you said?" she asked nonchalantly.

"A convertible Jag. Stereo, tape deck. No noisy kids spilling orange juice on you. No fight for the window seat. We both get one."

She shrugged her shoulders indifferently. "Okay. What time are you leaving? We don't want to arrive late."

"We'll soon catch up with the bus. There's no point going ahead of it. We can't check in till Mac gets there."

"We'd better tell Mac," Dawn said.

"You'll want to finish packing, too," Nick added. The minute the words were out he was afraid he'd blown the whole thing. She'd known he'd been in her room, and seen her partially packed suitcase. Incredibly, she didn't notice his gaffe.

"I didn't unpack anything but my dresses. You finish your coffee, Nick. I'll find Mac."

"I'll meet you in the parking lot around nine," he said.

"Right. Oh, maybe I should have my luggage taken on the bus. Your car probably has a tiny little trunk."

"Don't worry about that. I'll fit it in."

Dawn hopped up and went to the lobby. Mac was there, talking to Gloria Barker while they waited for the group to assemble and hand in their keys. Gloria had unbraided her hair and was wearing it loose, still kinked from last night. Either way, it looked fantastic. Mac seemed doubtful when Dawn told him her plan. "Do you think that's a good idea?" he asked. "You remember we discussed Barnaby last night. I think you're getting out of your league, Dawn."

She interpreted his remark to mean she was too young and naive to look after herself, and resented it. "Maybe you've misjudged my league," she said sharply, and turned away.

Gloria followed her. "I think Mac's right, Dawn," she said

But Gloria hadn't hesitated to go driving with Nick, Dawn thought. In fact, she'd asked him to take her to the hairdresser. Her comment sounded like sour grapes, and Dawn treated it accordingly. "It's my business, no one else's," she said.

"Suit yourself, but at least listen to what I have to say," Gloria persisted. "Nick isn't interested in you— or me, or anyone else on this tour. He's only interested in Hofstetter. He questions everyone he talks to about Hofstetter. Oh, he does it discreetly, but that's who he's interested in, all right. He didn't hit on you till I told him you sat beside Hofstetter on the bus."

"That's ridiculous! Why would he care about that?"

"I don't know, but I spoke to Mac about it, and it turns out Hofstetter didn't have a heart attack at all. He was arrested at customs. Two plainclothes Mounties took him away. They told Mac not to tell anyone. All very hush-hush. That's why Mac just announced that Hofstetter took a bad spell, but it wasn't serious."

Dawn listened to the story, unconvinced. "Why did he tell you then?" she asked.

"I told him Nick had been asking a lot of questions. It's *you* we're worried about, Dawn. If you know anything about Hofstetter's business, you should tell Mac.''

"I don't know anything about it, and I don't believe it, either," Dawn said angrily.

"If you ask me, it has something to do with smuggling drugs. I mean what else could it be? Nick wasn't one of the arresting officers. I think he's the guy Hofstetter was supposed to be selling the stuff to, and now he's out looking for it.''

Dawn listened, unable to believe this wild story. "How do you know the drugs weren't in Hofstetter's luggage? If he was smuggling anything, and I don't think he was, that's where they'd be. They didn't even search the luggage.''

"They took Hofstetter's bags off the bus," Gloria said. "Maybe they *did* find what they were looking for, and Nick is looking for something else—a list of names maybe. I don't know, but I don't think you should go with him.''

Gloria sounded sincere, and Dawn said, "Thanks for telling me. I'll think about it.''

"Think fast. We're leaving in fifteen minutes.''

Dawn hurried up to her room, her mind in turmoil. Nick, a drug smuggler? It was absurd. Gloria just didn't want any competition. Dawn inserted her key in the lock and rushed in. Whether she went with Nick or on the bus, she had to finish packing. She lifted her soft-sided case onto the bed and unzipped it. Her clothes looked as if they had just come out of the dryer. They were all jumbled together. She had placed the suitcase on its side on the floor so the contents wouldn't get mussed up. She had lifted it carefully for the same reason. How had everything gotten so disarranged?

The maid hadn't been in to do the room yet. Some-one had been searching her bag! Her fingers franti-cally sorted through to the bottom of the case, where she had her jewelry box hidden in a pair of socks. The case was loose. She opened it, breathing hard. It only held one good piece, her grandmother's gold heart-shaped locket with the seed pearl inset, but if it was gone....

The little gold heart on its chain fell into her fin-gers. She fastened it around her neck for safekeeping. The costume jewelry was all there. She took a quick look around the room. Nothing seemed to be gone, but she found other signs of an intruder. In the bath-room her plastic case of toilet articles had been un-zipped and the contents put in higgledy-piggledy. The soap box containing her nonallergenic soap wasn't closed properly. Whoever it was had been in a hurry. Luckily, she carried her money in her wallet.

Maybe the intruder had been in a hurry because he was already late for breakfast? So late he only had time for coffee—Nick? Good Lord, was Gloria right? Had she gotten involved with a drug dealer? Dawn took the case into the bedroom and sank on the edge of her bed, weak with shock and an incipient fear. Her hands were trembling. How could she have been such a dope? Of course Nick only chose her over Gloria because he wanted something from her. He thought Hofstetter had told her something, or given her something.

Nick *had* asked a lot of questions about Hofstetter. And furthermore, it was not only odd but downright unbelievable that a man like Nick would have joined this tour in the first place. He didn't know beans about history, and he probably hadn't been at the registry office last evening looking for his wallet. Where had he been? Out meeting with his colleagues probably. Maybe getting instructions. "Talk to the woman that was with Hofstetter on the bus. Make up to her, see what you can find out."

Anger seeped in by degrees and soon displaced her fear. Dawn jumped up purposefully and repacked her case. She picked it up and marched out of the room down to the lobby. She thought of reporting the break-in, but since nothing had been taken, there didn't seem any point in holding up the tour. She went up to Mac and said, "I'm going in the bus after all, Mac. Don't leave without me. I just want to have a word with Nick."

Mac used her words as an excuse to take her hand. "You're doing the right thing, Dawn," he said, with fatherly concern. "I was worried about you. Why don't you sit right up front with me today?"

Dawn was definitely not in the mood for a flirtation. She wanted to sit alone near the back and lick her wounds. "We'll see," she said, and went to the parking lot to look for Nick.

It was nearly time for the bus to leave, and while she didn't think Mac would leave without her, she didn't want to keep everyone waiting. She tapped her toe impatiently. Nick had said nine o'clock. Maybe she should phone his room. She started for the hotel, and at that moment he opened the door and came out. He was wearing his sunglasses and a blue, open-necked sport shirt. His white ducks added a final note of casual elegance. Dawn steeled herself against his good looks.

"I've changed my mind, Nick. I'm going on the bus," she said stiffly.

He slid his glasses down and peered at her over the top. "I suppose there's a reason?"

"I think you know the reason. But don't feel too badly. I don't know anything about Hofstetter and his drugs anyway, so you were wasting your time with me. Or had you figured that out already, when you searched my room this morning? No, of course you hadn't, or you wouldn't have asked me along for this joyride."

A scowl gathered on his brow and he said impatiently, "That's not why I asked you!"

"But you *are* checking up on Hofstetter!"

"Dawn, I've got to talk to you. Please, get in the car."

"With you? You must think I'm crazy!" She turned and stalked into the hotel.

In a fit of temper, Nick Barnaby balled his hands into fists and uttered a few expletives. How had she found out? Was it the mess he had made of her luggage? He had tried to tidy things up, but time had been short. Even if she'd found out he was the one in her room, how had she jumped to the conclusion that Hofstetter was involved? Who had told her? Someone on the tour obviously knew more than Dawn about all this. It must have been Mac. The Mounties had told him the truth, quite unnecessarily in Nick's opinion. Or had it been Gloria? She had been quite insistent on driving with him yesterday.

There wasn't much point following Dawn now and trying to change her mind in front of an audience. He'd have to wait till they got to Kingston. He got into his car and sat, thinking furiously.

Dawn managed to escape Mac and get a window seat near the rear of the bus for the short drive. Mr.

McDougall had somehow gotten away from his wife and girls and sat beside her in the aisle seat. He seemed to appreciate the quiet period, and didn't pester her with conversation. Dawn sat thinking as the scenery unfolded. The water gleamed gold and black. Along the highway there were some scraggly old pines but more maples and cedars. The surrounding farms and fields and houses looked very peaceful and bucolic. It was a shame to spoil the trip by thinking about Nick Barnaby, but she couldn't keep him out of her head.

The treacherous wretch. Giving her that mermaid, and joking about stealing her a paper flower. Stealing, he'd be good at that. His occupation explained his giving Mac a hundred-dollar tip. It explained the Jag he drove, too. A brand-new, shiny convertible. About the only thing she could say in his favor was that he hadn't attempted to seduce her. He called her innocent, and said he'd been "trying to do the right thing." What he meant was he didn't want her to get involved with a drug dealer. She had to admit there was one tiny speck of common decency still left in him.

If he hadn't thought she could tell him something about Hofstetter, he would have chosen Gloria for his partner. She'd be more his type. Dawn looked around the bus to see whom Gloria was with. Probably Herb, since she wasn't up front with Mac. Dawn spotted Herb, but he was with the shoe salesman from Syracuse. Where was Gloria? That blond head should be easy to find. Becoming curious, Dawn made a systematic search of every seat. Gloria wasn't there. Had the bus left without her?

Dawn became concerned and went up to speak to Mac. It was a difficult journey, picking her way up the aisle while the bus rocked from side to side, but she soon made it. "Mac, I don't see Gloria on the bus," she said.

Mac gave her a sheepish look. "She's coming with Barnaby," he said.

Dawn couldn't believe her ears. "With Barnaby!"

"She can handle him. He's too smooth for you, Dawn."

"She wouldn't go with him after what she told me!"

"What did she tell you?" he said. "That crazy idea she has about his being a drug dealer?"

"You thought so, too, didn't you?"

"I have no reason to think so," he said.

She lowered her voice and said, "But Hofstetter was arrested! What else could it be?"

"She wasn't supposed to tell anyone that! He wasn't exactly arrested, just taken into custody. He's not the drug-dealer type, an old guy like that. He might be in the country without a passport, or maybe he diddled some company books or something. You know white-collar crime. I didn't say Hofstetter's removal had anything to do with Barnaby. I figure he's just trying to pick up girls."

"Mr. Hofstetter did say he used to be an accountant," Dawn said doubtfully.

Mac gave her a teasing look. "It looks like Gloria finessed you, huh? Stole your seat in the Jag. She's good," he said, and laughed.

Dawn went back to her seat, so angry she wanted to strike someone. Gloria had looked so earnest and helpful when she was giving that line about Nick being a drug dealer. It had all sounded so convincing. Everything had seemed to back it up. Before long, though, Dawn realized that all the suspicious elements were still unexplained. Nick *had* searched her room. Why? If he was an ordinary thief, he certainly wouldn't have chosen the Pennypinchers' tour. He would have booked into some high-class hotel and worked anonymously, instead of mingling with his victims on an economy tour.

When Dawn looked out the window again, she noticed that the scenery had changed. The river had temporarily disappeared, and they were passing some large, institutional-looking gray stone buildings, with antique cannons in front. The sign said Old Fort Henry. Mac explained that it used to be a military fort, and was now a historical site and tourist attraction. They were slated to visit it that afternoon. They were getting close to Kingston. They crossed a bridge, and passed more limestone buildings on the left. These belonged to the Royal Military College, the Canadian version of West Point, Mac told them.

The bus continued into the city, heading south toward the river and their hotel. It stopped in front of one of the large buildings overlooking the water and everyone piled out. On the whole, Dawn preferred the more intimate Rockwood Manor to this anonymous skyscraper of steel and glass. While the group assembled in little clumps, Nick's black Jaguar pulled up. Gloria and he looked like models in a TV ad, with their windblown hair, tanned faces and dark glasses. Dawn glared for one instant, thinking, it could have been me! Then she purposefully turned her head away. Her heart was hammering with anger at Gloria's trick.

As soon as the luggage was taken off the bus, Dawn went into the hotel to claim her room. She didn't look around to see if Gloria and Nick had come in yet. She wouldn't have anything to do with them. They were a good pair; they deserved each other.

When everyone was present and checked in, Mac said, "We'll go to our rooms to freshen up and then regroup here in half an hour, for the morning's tour. Let's meet in the coffee shop, so the early arrivals can have something to drink. Okay?"

A murmur of assent ran through the group, and everyone headed for the elevators. Again Dawn was the first one on. From the rear, she saw Nick dash inside just as the door was about to close. Gloria missed the elevator by a few yards. Dawn turned aside and began talking to Mrs. McDougall.

"We're touring the waterfront this morning," she said. "The parks, a museum and a Martello tower."

"I wonder what a Martello tower is," Mrs. McDougall said. "Maybe Mr. Barnaby can tell us. He's a historian. I always say travel is so broadening. Mr. Barnaby!" She nudged her way forward and tugged at Nick's arm.

Lots of luck, Dawn thought to herself. He probably doesn't know a Martello tower from a marshmallow. The elevator stopped at the third floor and she got out, along with the shoe salesman. The group had rooms scattered all over the hotel as they had booked late. Mac had told Dawn that a feature of the Pennypincher tours was that they "picked up the empties" of first-class hotels at a discount rate. Dawn thought she and Mr. Kelly were the only two on this floor, till she heard footsteps behind them. She looked over her shoulder and saw Nick following, hurrying to catch up with them.

He gave her a nervous smile. "It looks like the three of us are going to be neighbors," he said in a hearty voice that sounded phony.

"I'm in Room 327," Mr. Kelly mentioned.

"And I'm in 329," Nick added. "How about you, Dawn?"

She gave him a cool stare. "I'm in 350. The far end of the hall," she said. Her key said 328, but she intended to walk right past that room. Nick could probably find out her number from the desk, but she wasn't going to make it easy for him. Mr. Kelly stopped at his room, Nick at his, and Dawn kept going. She turned the corner, then sneaked back to her room, being careful to make as little noise as possible when she opened the door. She peered across the hall when the key clicked. Nick's door opened a crack, then wider, and he stuck his head out.

He gave her a knowing smile. "I'm flattered," he said. "Did you change your room just to be near me?"

"I didn't change it."

He looked at the room number on the door. "Are you lost?" he asked, "or just doing a little breaking and entering?"

"I'll leave that up to you, but if you try to break into my room again, I'll report you to the police," she said.

"I only want to talk!"

Dawn closed her door. This time she didn't even wait to unpack her dresses, but just put her suitcase on the luggage rack and went back downstairs. She didn't want to be alone in that room for a minute. In fact, she was going to ask Mac to get her room changed to another floor.

She moved so quickly that she was the first one in the coffee shop. More coffee was the last thing she wanted, and she ordered a glass of orange juice, planning to nurse it till the others came. The first one down was Gloria Barker. The woman didn't even have the grace to blush at the trick she had pulled. She came right to Dawn's table and sat down, lifting her blond hair over her shoulder.

"I suppose you're wondering why I drove with Nick," she said.

"No, I'm not."

"Well, of course you are," Gloria said, in a voice that implied Dawn was a child. "I was just seeing if I could find out what he was up to. Mac and I figure you're too . . . inexperienced to handle him," she said, after searching for the right word.

Dawn didn't believe a word of it, but she didn't plan to have an argument over Nick either. "Did you learn much?" she asked.

"He denied the whole thing. I suppose I could be wrong about him," she said uncertainly. "Mac doesn't believe it. If he's innocent—well, he's awfully cute." She smiled.

"Before you decide to marry him, Gloria, maybe you'd better listen to what I have to say. I don't know what Nick Barnaby is up to, but he *is* up to something. He broke into my room at Rockwood Manor and searched it this morning."

Gloria's big blue eyes grew wider. "You're kidding! Did he take anything?"

"No. Nothing was missing."

"Why would he do that?" Gloria looked very skeptical.

"You're on such good terms, why don't you ask him? I'd like to hear the answer myself."

Others from their tour began sifting into the coffee shop. It was a busy place, and they sat wherever they could find a seat. Gloria moved to another table.

Dawn noticed that Nick was once again the last to arrive. She was surprised he had come at all. She turned her head away as soon as she spotted him, and didn't look in his direction till the group was leaving.

"We walk the next lap, folks," Mac announced. "I hope you're all wearing comfortable shoes. It's a beautiful day, it's not that far and you'll see more on foot. So, are we all ready?"

He headed for the lobby, with the group following behind. The streets were full of people and it was a warm day. The sun was climbing, and the temperature was already uncomfortably high. Dawn decided to tag along at the rear of the group, so she could keep an eye on Nick. He was with Gloria again. Their smiles and chatter indicated that he had either squelched her fears, or talked her into accepting a criminal.

Dawn tried to rouse herself to interest at the museum and the tour of the Martello tower. She and everyone else finally found out what the Martello tower was. It was a round guardhouse erected around 1812, during the British-American war. It was apparently modeled after towers erected in England to look out for and ward off Napoleon's invasion. It had little slits of windows designed to allow a gun to shoot at attackers, and a walkway around the top for a better view of the horizon. The enemy would come from the south by boat. It seemed unreal to Dawn that America and Canada, who now claimed the longest undefended border in the world, had ever been enemies.

The scenery was pretty, and Dawn enjoyed a ride on a little red mini double-decker bus, but by twelve-thirty, she was glad the tour of Kingston was over, and they were returning to the hotel.

"Lunch is at one," Mac announced. "There's an open-air patio overlooking the river. Shall we have something cold to drink? The paddle steamer is just loading up. It's worth a look to see it in motion. If you're interested, you can take the late-afternoon trip when we come back from Fort Henry, or you can take the evening cruise—not included in the tour."

A drink on the patio at least met with unanimous approval. Dawn surreptitiously looked to see where Nick was sitting, so she could seat herself far away. He had become detached from Gloria during the morning. She was back with Herb, and Nick was with Miss Edmonds and her group. That annoyed Dawn, too. She got along better with Miss Edmonds than anyone else in the group. And to top it all off, she got stuck sitting with the McDougalls.

"I want an ice cream cone," Fiona announced.

"You'll have fruit juice or milk, and like it," her mother scolded. "Look at the big boat, girls. It's called a paddle steamer."

"The paddle isn't moving. I want a soft drink," Flora said in a loud, whining voice.

"We'll make that two glasses of milk," Mrs. McDougall told her husband.

"We're on holiday. Marion. A soft drink won't hurt them," he said gently.

"And I suppose *you're* planning to have a beer," she said in her waspish way.

"Just coffee for me," he said mildly, but he stuck to his guns and ordered soft drinks for the girls.

"I'll have an iced tea," Dawn told the waiter. She didn't really want anything, but it was nice on the patio, and she felt she should order something since she was taking up a seat. The umbrella wasn't large enough to cover them all, and she pulled out her sun-screen to put some on her exposed arms. They were already a little pink from the morning's walk.

Across the patio, a thin, pale-faced man in a white shirt watched Dawn. When she reached for her bag, he craned his neck forward, watching intently. One of the little girls blocked his view, but he'd seen the big canvas bag, just as Werfel had described.

Nick Barnaby, glancing around the crowd from behind his dark glasses, noticed the man, and the direction he was looking. Of course Dawn was attractive. The man might be ogling her for that reason. That annoyed him, too. The stranger was much too old for one thing, and too ugly for another.

Most of the other guests were looking at the paddle steamer. It was loaded, but it didn't leave its berth. Everyone kept watching, waiting for the moment when the wheel would begin to churn the water, calling up memories of riverboat gamblers and the old South. The passengers on board waited, too, waving. Fiona and Flora squabbled all through the half hour.

"My drink's sour," Fiona complained.

"You should have ordered milk," her mother replied.

"It tastes awful!" Fiona shoved it away, and the light paper cup tipped over. A rivulet of syrupy orange drink sloshed across the table onto Dawn's skirt.

"Now see what you've done," Mrs McDougall scolded. "I'm sorry, Miss Roberts. It won't stain if you get water on it right away. It'll soon dry in this heat. These girls are impossible. Say you're sorry, Fiona."

"It's all right," Dawn said, and picked up her bag. "I'll just rinse it out."

Chapter Five

When Dawn stood up, Nick watched her closely. Then he turned and looked at the thin man in the white shirt. He was still watching her, too, not in an obvious way, but discreetly. Nick frowned.

Dawn rose and went toward the hotel, trying to decide whether to change her skirt or just sponge it off. The stain wasn't very big, and as her skirt was full, it didn't show much. At the edge of the patio, she stopped to get her bearings. She wasn't sure how to get into the hotel from there. The patio was a story below the front entrance. The only door seemed to lead into the kitchen, which was marked Employees Only. There had to be a washroom nearby, since drinks were served on the patio. She asked a waitress, and the woman said, "Just through that gate there, and to your left. You can't miss it."

On the patio, the man in the white shirt casually drew out his wallet and put some money into the little tray on the table. He rose slowly and sauntered away. Nick watched to see which way he went. He followed the same route Dawn had taken. Nick had already checked it out, and knew it led eventually to the main street and the stores. If the man was a local, he might be leaving that way.

Nick drew out his wallet and looked for a small bill. Wouldn't you know it, he didn't have anything smaller than a twenty. "Mary, would you be a doll and take my change when the waitress comes back," he said, handing Miss Edmonds the bill.

"I think I can change that for you, Nick." She opened her purse and began pulling out money.

Nick watched as Dawn disappeared through a gate, with the man a few yards behind her. He was probably being overly cautious, but it was possible Dawn was in danger. "Don't bother. Just take this," he said, and pushed the twenty at Miss Edmonds.

Nick hurried across the patio, dodging tables and waitresses. As he passed Mac Sempleton's table, Mac put out a hand and stopped him. "You were wondering about parking your car, Nick."

"Yeah, later."

Mac was still holding on to him. "It won't take a minute. I was just going to tell you I spoke to the clerk, and he said you can put it in the hotel garage, but you'll have to pay extra. Our rate doesn't include parking. I'd do it if I were you. There are a lot of kids hanging around the parking lot, and that Jag is a temptation."

"Thanks, Mac," Nick said, and hurried on. His worry was swiftly mounting, and in his mad dash he bumped into a waitress, and a tray of drinks went flying through the air. "I'm sorry!" he said, and automatically began helping her pick the glasses up. But there wasn't time. "I have to go," he said distractedly. "I'll be back." She probably thought he was a moron or an uncouth lout, but he had a very unpleasant feeling at the bottom of his gut that something was wrong.

Dawn decided she'd just sponge out the stain, to save a trip upstairs. She went through the gate, along a paved walk. It was cool in the shade of the tall building. Geraniums nestled among the silvery velvet plumes of dusty miller along the edge of the path. Between the path and the hotel there was a patch of grass and ornamental shrubs. On the other side, the fence cut off the noise from the patio. It was so quiet she could hear some birds chirping, and she looked up to spot them.

Dawn was standing, clutching her heavy bag with one hand and looking for the birds, when the blow fell. She hadn't heard anyone behind her. The attack came out of the blue, and it didn't even hurt much at first. She was stunned, but not completely unconscious, and was aware of the man pulling at her bag. She tried to hold on, to fight him, but everything was fuzzy, and her fingers felt limp. He wrenched the bag from her and pushed her back. In her weakened state, she fell easily. From her position flat on the ground, she saw the sky, and just barely heard retreating footsteps. But why hadn't she noticed him come up behind her? He must have been wearing soft-soled shoes. It had all happened so fast and so unexpectedly that it seemed unreal. She hadn't even called for help.

She struggled to her feet. When she stood up, the whole world seemed to turn in circles. The sky and the grass and glass windows of the hotel were all one whirling mass dotted with fiery red spots. She closed her eyes for a moment. Then the pain in her temple began, not throbbing, but a hard, dull ache. When she opened her eyes, the world had settled down to normal.

My purse! My two hundred dollars! I've got to stop him, she thought, and hurried along the path to the corner, where it made a sharp left turn. She looked and saw where her big canvas purse had been tossed into a stand of ornamental mock orange bushes. She hurried toward the bushes, certain that her wallet would be gone. The purse was gaping open and completely empty. Under the bushes, she saw her little tan leather cosmetics bag and the package of paper tissues. She got down on her hands and knees and searched, finding more items hiding beneath low-lying branches. The colored cover of her paperback novel was easy to spot. And right beneath it was her black leather wallet, well used and worn around the edges.

She picked it up joyfully, hardly able to believe her luck. It hadn't even been opened. She unfastened the clasp and saw that all her money was there, the Canadian bills that seemed strange to her, with odd colors. The five was blue, the ten purple, with pictures of the queen and old prime ministers whose names she didn't know. She looked on the ground again and gathered up the last of her belongings. Everything seemed to be there. At the sound of running footsteps, she turned around and saw Nick hurrying along the path.

He noticed with a great flood of relief that Dawn was alone, and he thought, unharmed. The man hadn't been following her, after all. Like an anxious parent after a child has misbehaved in some dangerous way, Nick felt his released anxiety turn to anger. "You shouldn't go wandering off alone!" he exclaimed harshly. "You might get hurt."

Dawn stared at him mutely, and as he drew closer, he saw that she was ghost white. Her eyes looked like two big, dark pools. "I was," she said. "I—I was attacked. A purse snatcher...hit me...." Her voice was feeble, and she was weaving back and forth, as if she might faint.

Anger at himself filled his heart. If anything had happened to her, it would have been his fault! He should have told her what was going on. He rushed forward and drew her into his arms. "Oh my God! Are you all right?" She felt small and fragile, vulnerable. He could feel the trembling that shook her, and held her more closely. A fierce tenderness came over Nick as he stood, gently stroking her back and soothing her fears. One corner of his mind noticed that the attacker hadn't gotten her purse away from her. Whoever it was must have been Hofstetter's accomplice.

He wanted to chase the man, but Dawn was too shaken to be left alone. And besides, whoever had attacked her would be long gone by now. "I'll take you to your room," he said. "Do you want me to call a doctor?"

"The police would be more appropriate," she said. As her fears subsided, Dawn became angry at the assault. "The trouble is, I don't have a single idea what he looked like. Or even whether it was a man or a woman."

"It was a man," Nick said grimly. "I saw him. A tall, skinny guy in a white shirt. I can give them a description, not that it'll do much good. We'll get you to your room first. Maybe a cold compress would help."

Nick put his arm around her waist and led her into the hotel. Her head was aching, but as the pain lessened, she began to think more clearly. She noticed that Nick was wearing loafers with leather soles. Most of the group wore sneakers, which wouldn't have made any sound, either. But it was odd that Nick had shown up so quickly after the attack. Had he been following her? She realized that he might have been the one who had hit her. He hadn't found what he wanted in her room, so he had stolen her purse. Of course he wouldn't admit it. And she wouldn't admit she suspected him, either, not till she had other people around to protect her. People—that was what she wanted.

"I'd really like something cold to drink, Nick," she said. Her voice sounded unsteady, but her ordeal could account for that. "Let's stop at the coffee shop."

He looked surprised. "We can have something brought up to your room. You'll be more comfortable lying down."

And easier to knock out and tie up. "I'd rather stay downstairs," was all she said, and they went to the coffee shop.

At the lunch hour, there wasn't a table to be had. Nick got the soft drinks and they went to the lobby, which gave them a sort of privacy amid the confusion. "We'd better call the police now," Dawn suggested when she had recovered a little bit.

"Why don't we tell the house detective first?" Nick suggested. "The hotel will be concerned that one of their clients was attacked, and he can make the report to the police. You really look as if you should be in bed." Nick's expression was concerned, worried. But then she already knew he was a good actor. "I'll stick around and talk to the police when they come. I'm the one who saw the man, and can give a description."

Dawn pretended to agree. She'd talk to the police privately as well, and air her suspicions about Nick. It would be her word against his, since there wasn't a shred of proof. Nick went to look for the house detective, and Dawn waited and continued to think furiously. It was a lousy trick to play on Nick if he was innocent, but it had to be him. There couldn't be two men that eager to search her belongings.

"Dawn, there you are!" Miss Edmonds exclaimed. The tour group was coming into the hotel, ready for their lunch. "I was beginning to worry about you. I thought Nick was with you. I think he was anxious when he saw you leave, and that man got up and followed you. He didn't say anything, but I had a feeling he was upset, the way he dashed off without waiting for his change."

"You saw a man follow me?" Dawn exclaimed.

"Yes, a tall thin man. He had on a white shirt. He didn't—I hope nothing happened!"

Dawn was aware of a very pleasant, warm sensation washing through her. It wasn't Nick! He had been telling the truth. It wasn't till that moment that she realized how very much she had disliked suspecting Nick. He had been watching over her, trying to protect her. Whatever was going on—and obviously there was something irregular afoot—Nick was on her side.

"I was attacked by a purse snatcher," she announced, managing a wobbly smile.

"I guess you must have caught him, from that grin you've got."

"No, he ran away, but Nick's reporting it to the house detective now."

"I'll tell Mac to warn the group. You're not safe anywhere nowadays," Miss Edmonds replied. "Will you and Nick be coming for lunch?"

"Oh yes, we'll be there." Her head only ached a little bit now. She felt light, giddy with relief.

Miss Edmonds went along with the rest of the group and Dawn waited for Nick. When he returned, he had a man in a gray business suit with him. He was a big bruiser with brown hair turning gray around the temples. He looked like an ex-cop. Nick introduced him as Mr. Francis, the house detective. Mr. Francis was blasé about an attack in which nothing was stolen, and no one was seriously hurt. He wrote the details on a little pad. "I'll report this to the police," he said. "If they want to ask any questions, they'll be in touch. How long are you folks here for?"

"Just till tomorrow morning," Nick told him.

"Then you probably won't be hearing from them, but I'll file the report. We have the description, that's the main thing. I can get your home addresses from the desk if we need to be in touch with you later. I'll let you folks have your lunch now." He stuck his little pad and pen in his pocket and left.

"Do you feel up to lunch?" Nick asked. He noticed that Dawn was looking much better. In fact, she seemed strangely elated about something.

"I'm starved. And we have the tour of Fort Henry this afternoon, so we'd better eat."

Nick stared at her, astonished. "Do you think you're up to it? I thought you'd want to rest."

"I'm not tired. Let's go."

He went with her, but his old suspicions were re-awakening at her strange behavior. How had she recovered so quickly? And why was she in this excited mood, as if she'd just scored some kind of coup? Was it possible he'd just been conned by a pair of clever thieves? How could Dawn not have gotten a look at her attacker. Maybe she didn't want to identify him, because he was her colleague.

Perhaps she hadn't been attacked at all. They'd arranged to meet for her to hand over the contraband. She had been pretty quick to squash Nick's suggestion of calling a doctor. She really had looked pale when he first saw her, but that might have been fear that he'd seen her and her colleague making the exchange. Her story that nothing was taken from her purse sounded extremely unlikely, too, once his eyes were opened. Her insistence on joining the others—that could have been a ruse to avoid answering some questions. He wouldn't let on he suspected anything, but before long, Dawn Roberts was going to have to answer some hard questions.

When they joined the others, Dawn was the center of attention. Miss Edmonds had spread the story of the attack on her, and Dawn described in vivid detail how she hadn't heard a single sound behind her. The man had stolen her purse and scattered all her belongings to the wind, without taking a thing. And Nick had rescued her. Nick came in for his share of praise.

"Why did he attack you then?" Gloria asked. "He must have seen your wallet. That's what a purse snatcher would be after."

"He must have seen Nick coming. I guess Nick scared him off," Dawn suggested, with a soft, admiring smile at her companion.

It was the kind of smile that made a man's chest swell, and his ego blossom. Nick sat, trying to keep the edge of cynicism from his expression. Some brave rescue! She was standing alone, with her purse intact, when he got there.

Hofstetter had chosen his accomplice well. No one looking at Dawn would suspect those big green eyes and that freckled little nose of anything crooked. She looked as innocent as Hofstetter himself, with his unfashionable, steel-rimmed glasses, his old, rumpled suit and his fatherly manner. Who was she really? A relative, maybe? Lots of Pennsylvania Dutch, which is what Hofstetter was in Scranton.

Nick's thoughts wandered, and when he tuned into the conversation again, he heard Dawn say, "The house detective didn't seem very interested. I think the matter is closed."

She'd like that, but as far as Nick was concerned, the matter was far from closed. It had just taken a new twist. It would be interesting to see how she behaved when he gave her a clue that she wasn't home free. Dawn was the only lead he had now. The man in the white shirt might have gotten away with the contraband, but Dawn must know where and who he was, and, by God, he'd get it out of her somehow.

When lunch was over, Nick said, "Are you really well enough to tour Fort Henry? You shouldn't overexert yourself after that ordeal this morning."

He sounded concerned, and had never looked more irresistible. She gave him an admiring smile. "Did you have something else in mind?" she asked. Dawn was more than willing to pass on the tour for a chance to be alone with Nick.

She was good! Just the right air of innocent reluctance, but not enough to discourage him—by any means. "I thought a relaxing drive along the river might be better for you. I was looking at the map. There's a place called the Bath Road that runs along the river. There should be some nice scenery."

"It sounds lovely. Maybe a tour is too strenuous today. And I'll finally get a ride in that Jag you're always bragging about," she added, laughing.

"A window seat," he agreed. "Have I really been bragging? How uncool of me."

"I guess I'd brag too if I had a car like that. I have to drive the Gourmet Kitchen van when I need a car. Talk about uncool. It smells like shrimp. Shrimp puffs are our best seller."

Nick thought she was overdoing the simple hick act a little, but he made a joking reply. "I'll tell Mac we're taking the afternoon off," he said.

The crowd was dispersing and Nick went to look for Mac. When Dawn stood up, she noticed the stain on her skirt from Fiona's spilled drink, and decided to change. She looked in her purse for her room key, and couldn't find it. Either the man who searched her purse had taken it, or she had lost it in the bushes. She had looked all around the ground. He must have taken it. And if he had, he obviously intended to search her room. Maybe he was there right now! She was afraid to go up alone, and waited till Nick came back, grateful that he was there to help her.

She ran to meet him, her eyes wide. "Nick, the worst thing! My key's missing. Maybe the man who attacked me stole it. Will you come up to my room with me? He might be there now."

Nick hesitated a moment. Was this some kind of trick? A guy waiting to crack him over the head? No, what would be the point of that? She was just trying to give a reason for that apparently pointless attack. It was a stupid mistake not to let on her wallet was stolen. "Missing?" he asked, playing for time. "When did you lose it?"

"I don't know. Maybe I just left it in my room, but I'm kind of afraid to go up alone."

"We'll have a look then," he said.

Dawn chattered away as they went up in the elevator. "You know, it could be the man's a sex maniac. That would explain why he didn't steal my wallet—because he plans to sneak into my room tonight and attack me. Boy, I thought Mom was exaggerating when she told me to be careful. If my key's not there, I'm going to get my room changed."

Now she was dragging in "Mom." Next she'd be waving the flag and asking for apple pie. Nick schooled his features to concern and said, "We'll certainly have to get you out of that room."

When they got to the door, he let Dawn go in first, while he took a good look around. He peered through the crack where the door hinged and saw that no one was hiding. In the mirror, he examined the far side of the room. The bathroom was the only place the man could be, and he entered warily. The bathroom door was open a crack.

Dawn had done no more than walk into her room and put her suitcase on the rack that morning, so it didn't take much looking to discover that the key wasn't there. "He got it! That's what he was after!" Dawn said, feeling weak at her narrow escape.

Nick looked at the bathroom door. It hadn't moved. "Why don't you change your skirt, and we'll speak to the desk about changing your room?"

"I won't be a minute." Dawn unlocked her suitcase and shook out a denim skirt. Before she went into the bathroom to change, she went to Nick and took his hand. "I'm so glad you're here, Nick. I feel—safe with you."

Nick fought down the urge to throttle that innocent smile off her face. He squeezed her fingers and said, "You can consider me your personal guardian angel, Dawn."

"Guard the door," she said, and picked up her purse. "I'll try to do something to my face, too," she added before whisking into the bathroom. He took a look when she opened the door and saw that the room was empty.

Did she think he was going to search her purse? Was that why she felt obliged to make that explanation for taking it with her? He knew there wouldn't be anything in the purse now that her colleague had met her.

After Dawn changed her skirt, she opened the bag and looked for her sunscreen. For an afternoon in an open car she would definitely require another coat. The bottle was gone, but obviously her attacker hadn't been after her sunscreen. She half remembered leaving it on the patio table. Maybe Mrs. McDougall had picked it up. She'd try to catch her before the bus left. Dawn applied fresh lipstick and brushed out her hair, trying vainly to get some order into her springy curls. The humidity always defeated her.

"All set," she announced when she came out.

"Your guardian angel is waiting," he replied. "He does double duty as a porter." He picked up her case and they left.

In the elevator, Dawn said, "I'll arrange about my room change while you bring around the car. It'll save time."

"You just can't wait to get into that convertible, huh?" he joked, to keep up his pretense of goodwill.

Dawn went to the desk. The house detective had told the clerk about Miss Roberts's attacker, and the man didn't give her any trouble about a room change. In fact, he was very solicitous. The room wouldn't be vacant till checkout time, however, so he kept her bag at the desk.

"Has the bus tour left for Fort Henry yet?" Dawn asked.

"It just pulled out. I hope you weren't planning to take it?"

"No, I just wanted to speak to someone, but it's not important."

She nipped into the little convenience shop in the hotel and got a small tube of sunscreen. She applied it to her face and arms before joining Nick. Her vanity didn't like making an issue of her freckles in front of him. When she went out the front door, the shiny black Jag was waiting for her. It was going to be a wonderful afternoon, just her and Nick, driving along in the open car with the sun shining. The doorman opened the door, and she hopped in, feeling as pampered as a princess.

"To Bath Road, James," she said, and leaned back against the tan leather seat. "Boy, this is what I call luxury. Do you know the way?"

"I studied the map while I was waiting for you. Did you get your room changed all right?"

"No problem. They were very nice about it. Everyone's being very nice." She put on her sunglasses and breathed an exultant sigh of pleasure.

Nick turned the key, the powerful engine purred and they were off. The busy waterfront area was clogged with traffic, and Dawn enjoyed the envious stares she and Nick were given. It wasn't often she had the chance to play such a glamorous role. Once they were out of town, it was even more exciting. When the car picked up speed on a less-traveled road, the wind grabbed her hair and pulled it back. Her blouse was plastered against her body, and the noise was loud.

"I didn't know it would be so breezy," she said, raising her voice so he could hear her. "I should have worn a kerchief."

Nick just turned his head toward her and smiled behind his dark glasses. She decided it was the dark glasses that gave his smile that vaguely menacing air. Maybe she looked menacing too. She grinned. It was ironic to think of her scaring anyone.

"What are you laughing at?" Nick asked.

"I was just wondering if you're afraid of me."

"Scared stiff," he said. "Should I be? Are you carrying a gun?"

"No. Are you?"

"Should I be?" he asked.

Conversation was a little difficult in the windy car, and they just drove on, till they were in the country. Houses were farther apart there. At some points, the road cut close to the river, leaving no room for buildings. "Shall we stop and walk a little?" Nick suggested.

"Sure. We'll go down to the water and wade. We should have brought our bathing suits."

"Here's a place just ahead." Nick pulled off on a wide shoulder and parked the car. A tumble of big boulders led down to the water. Nearby, drooping willows spread their branches, giving shade and coolness. There was a beach of smooth stones below, with water lapping gently over it. They got out and Nick helped Dawn over the rocks. She was as light as a feather when he lifted her bodily over the last drop. It angered him that this slip of a girl was making a monkey of him.

"It's strange, finding isolated spots like this so close to a city," Dawn mentioned. "We could be in the middle of a wilderness, except for the boats out there." She shaded her eyes and gazed across the peaceful water to where a few fishing boats and pleasure craft bobbed on the rippled surface.

Nick glanced at the boats and decided they were too far from shore to hear if Dawn shouted. He looked up, and checked that they weren't visible from the road. Then he turned to Dawn and said, "It's time for our talk now."

Unsuspecting, Dawn said, "What do you want to talk about?"

"For starters, why don't you tell me how you got into this?" He reached out, removed her sunglasses and stuck them in his shirt pocket. He wanted to see her eyes when she began her tale. He could usually tell whether a person was lying by the eyes.

She blinked in surprise, and Nick realized it was all a myth, about reading a person's eyes. She looked as innocent as a baby.

"What are you talking about?" she asked.

"You, Hofstetter, the man you met this morning."

His voice had taken on a menacing tone, and shivers of fear began scuttling up her spine. Dawn's throat felt dry, and she stepped back, away from him. He reached out and seized her wrists in a firm grip.

"I don't know what you're talking about," Dawn finally managed. "I just met Hofstetter once, and I didn't meet any man this morning. I was attacked."

Nick was impatient and dropped any pretense of politeness. "Did he get them?" he demanded in a harsh voice. His fingers tightened on her wrists.

Her fear quickly mounted to terror. Those dark glasses that hid his eyes had something to do with it. She felt she didn't know Nick Barnaby at all. He had become a sinister stranger. "Get what?" she asked in a breathless voice.

"You know what I'm talking about," he barked. "You had them. They weren't on Hofstetter, and they weren't on the bus. I even went back and checked the ground at customs. He took them on the bus with him. The only person he talked to was you. Cut the baloney, Dawn. You're not getting out of here till you tell me where they are."

While he talked, his grip on her had loosened. Dawn took advantage of it and jerked her hands free. Nick reached out to grab her again. In a split second, she had taken to her heels and fled down the rough, pebbled beach. The footing was treacherous, and to add to her frustration, a wall of rock stretched into the water not twenty yards away. He'd catch her if she tried to scramble up to the highway. She heard him gaining on her, and before she could think what to do, he had caught her. His hand reached out and pulled her arm, spinning her around.

She looked into his face, and was confronted once again with those impenetrable sunglasses. Beneath them, his lips were grim, and he was panting from the chase. His fingers felt like manacles on her wrists. "Start talking," he growled.

Dawn's eyes looked black with fear. That sprinkle of freckles stood out against her blanched face. He had never seen anyone look so terrified in his life, and in spite of his determination, Nick feared he was being too rough on her. She was just a kid, after all. Hofstetter was using her. "You could be in a lot of trouble if you don't come clean, Dawn," he said, less harshly.

"I don't know what you're talking about. *You're* the one who's been acting fishy. If you're a drug dealer—"

Nick's jaw fell an inch. "A drug dealer!"

"Well, what else could it be? If Hofstetter was smuggling something—oh, I know he was stopped at customs. Mac told Gloria. But he didn't give it to me."

"He wasn't a drug dealer!"

"What was he then?"

"He's a jewel thief. He was smuggling diamonds out of the States. *My* diamonds."

Dawn was momentarily speechless. Diamonds! *Nick's* diamonds. Then Nick wasn't a drug dealer, or a thief, or anything evil. "Oh, I'm so glad," she said, and to her dismay, she giggled in sheer relief.

Nick just looked. She could always surprise him. This slip of a kid, not up to his chin, was standing there, giggling at his loss of three million dollars, worth of diamonds. "I'm glad you're amused," he said in a chilly voice. "But maybe you could stop laughing long enough to help me."

Chapter Six

Dawn was chagrined when he accused her of laughing at him. "I'm sorry, Nick," she said. "It was what my mom calls a funeral laugh. You know, the inappropriate kind that just comes over you sometimes from nerves or anxiety or relief. Of course I wasn't laughing at you. How can I help?"

Now why should he feel like a brute? He hadn't done anything, except threaten her a little. "For starters," he said, "you can let me search the pockets of those brown shorts you were wearing when you sat beside Hofstetter on the bus. I figure he must have slipped the diamonds in there when he saw the bus stopping at customs."

Dawn wrinkled her brow in concentration and said, "No, he didn't. Is that what you were looking for when you searched my room—my shorts?"

"Yes, but I couldn't find them. Where the devil did you put them anyway?"

"In a plastic laundry bag the hotel provided. I kept it in the shower stall so my room wouldn't look messy, but the diamonds weren't there."

"He might have been carrying them in a little bag, or have them wrapped in a paper tissue or something," Nick explained. "Three million dollars' worth of diamonds doesn't make a big parcel. You might have missed it."

"My khaki shorts don't have any pockets," she said simply.

"Oh." Boy, he was some clever detective. He hadn't thought of that. "Damn. I was sure that was it. I figure Hofstetter was afraid he'd be recognized when they made everyone get off the bus. He was very eager to get those diamonds out of the country, and I thought he'd palm them off on someone. They're hotter than the fires of hell."

"How did you come to have so many diamonds, Nick? Are you a jeweler or something?" Dawn inquired.

"Not exactly, but we handle a lot of diamonds. My mother is a jewelry designer. She creates original, one-of-a-kind pieces. She used to sell them to her friends, but as her reputation grew, the business grew along with it and she opened her own shop. Mom doesn't do all the designing now, but she still does special pieces for old customers. Dad used to run the business. When he died, I took it over. I'm no artist, I handle the business end of the company."

She gave him a laughing look. "I didn't think you were a history professor."

"That was another mistake," he admitted ruefully, "claiming to know anything about history, when there was a bunch of schoolteachers in the group."

"What's your store called?"

"Mom uses her maiden name—Verely. You probably haven't heard of us. We're not exactly in the Tiffany league, but we have an exclusive international clientele. Mom gets assignments from all over—Europe and Asia, as well as America. She had a meeting in London with an old lady, a countess actually, who had been hoarding marvelous gems for years. The countess needed cash for taxes and decided to sell some of her unmounted diamonds. She knows Mom, and offered them to her directly, to save the commission. Mom went to a hotel in London to meet the countess and assess the stones. She bought the whole lot of them. Mom had them in her hotel room after the countess left. She planned to put them in the hotel safe overnight and take an early flight home the next morning. It didn't quite work out that way," he said, and sighed.

Dawn listened, spellbound. "She was robbed right in the hotel?" she asked when he paused.

"Someone obviously followed the countess. Her collection is well-known, and I imagine it had leaked out that she was trying to sell the diamonds. If only they had got to her before we took possession! As it is, Verely is the loser. There hadn't even been time to get the stones insured."

"That's terrible, Nick. I'm surprised your mother would go alone on a trip like that. Why didn't she hire a guard, when she knew she'd be carrying such valuable things?"

Nick gave Dawn a sheepish look. "Why should she, when she has an able-bodied son? I was with her. I was on my way to the elevator to take the diamonds to the hotel safe when I was attacked. A door in the hall opened and a man came out. I never knew what hit me. But I did get a quick glance at the man."

Dawn felt Nick slipping ever farther away from her. His life-style, meeting with countesses, buying millions of dollars' worth of diamonds—what chance would she have with him? "Who was he? Hofstetter?" she asked, drawing her attention back to his story.

"Not in person, but one of his ring. Of course we notified Scotland Yard immediately and I was given a book of mug shots to look through. I identified the man, and when Scotland Yard got in touch with Interpol, they fingered him as one of Hofstetter's boys. It's an international ring. Hofstetter's ring," he finished grimly. "Of course that's not his real name. It's Gerhart Werfel. He runs a band of old pros, who have been operating ever since the war. That's World War II I'm talking about. Last week Interpol notified us that Werfel had slipped out of England on a forged passport, headed for the States, but they didn't think he'd try to unload the stones there. Some of them are quite distinctive. The countess collected rare and unique gems. Of course Interpol notified the RCMP here in Canada."

"And you figure Hofstetter headed to Canada?" Dawn asked.

He nodded. "It's a little out of the major diamond market, but there are enough jewelers in Toronto that he could sell the stones. Interpol checked the airports, so we knew he hadn't flown out of the States. He had used the ruse of joining a tour group once before, in France. After a lot of investigating, someone at Pennypincher's Travel recognized his face from a picture."

Dawn listened closely, and said, "If the stones are unique and he tries to sell them, they'll be recognized, and you can catch him."

"We might, if he deals with a legitimate buyer, which he probably won't. He might recut them, though that would lower their value considerably."

Dawn puzzled over the matter a moment. "Why isn't Interpol here, if they've been doing all this investigating?"

"They are. Gloria Barker."

Dawn's mouth opened wide, and a sound like a frightened mouse came out of it. "Gloria! You mean that bleach—that—"

"That very intelligent lady has been helping me. Or rather I've been helping her."

Dawn found it easier to believe that Nick was a diamond king than to believe that Gloria was an Interpol agent. "But she lied to me! Why did she tell me you were a drug dealer, and warn me to keep away from you?"

"Gloria wanted to come with me in the car this morning—so we could make plans," he added hastily. "She decided you were getting in our way, and wanted to scare you off. She didn't tell me she'd called me a drug dealer," he added angrily.

Dawn was angry with Gloria, too. "I don't suppose she approves of our being together now, either," she snapped.

"Since you were attacked, she agrees with me that you might be the carrier unwittingly. She's not on the tour this afternoon. She's out beating the bushes for clues. But you know, you've been getting in her way since day one. She was supposed to nab the seat beside Werfel, but you beat her to it."

Dawn tossed her head in annoyance. "So you decided to charm the truth out of me by pretending you liked me." That was all it amounted to. Nick didn't care a fig for her.

Nick read her expression and tried to conciliate her. "And failed, but *you* charmed the truth out of *me*," he pointed out. "So now we can quit pretending and be friends. And by the way, what I've been telling you isn't exactly public knowledge, Dawn. I'd appreciate it if you didn't say anything to the others. Especially to Gloria. She's in charge."

"I suppose I should do whatever I can to help catch the criminals," she said, to let him know it wasn't his "charm" that had swayed her. "It's only right. Okay, mum's the word."

They stood a moment, looking at the drifting river, while they pondered the problem. The isolation of the spot began to make Dawn nervous. "Anybody could see your car parked at the side of the road, Nick. Maybe we should go some place more secure."

"That's not a bad idea. Wer—Hofstetter's colleague seems to have the idea that you've got the diamonds, and he plays rough. We passed a little inn a mile back. Let's go there and talk."

The inn was called the Royal Arms. It had a stretch of private beach for its guests, and tables with red-and-white-striped umbrellas set out on a patio. Dawn and Nick ordered a beer and discussed the problem.

"Hofstetter was allowed a phone call when he was taken into custody," Nick said. "Gloria figures he got some message through via his lawyer as to what he did with the diamonds. Since his friend attacked you, it looks like you're it, Dawn. I know your purse has already been ransacked, but maybe we should go through it again with a fine-tooth comb."

She placed the big canvas bag on the table. "Root away. The man who searched it didn't take anything but my hotel key, so if I had the diamonds, they're still here."

She began placing the old familiar items on the table. Nick opened the cosmetics bag first. He examined her lipstick and hair brush, her little compact mirror and tube of mascara. He shook everything and even felt the lining of the bag. Next he took the package of paper tissues and removed each one.

"Unless he crushed the stones to powder, you can feel that they're not in there," she objected, and stuffed the tissues back.

He took her tube of sunscreen and felt it. "Don't squeeze it all out! They're not in there. I just bought it at the hotel here in Kingston. Try this," she said, and handed him her paperback.

He smiled at the cover of the romantic novel. Dawn might try to pretend she was all business, but that book told him otherwise. "Even I'm not enough of an optimist to think diamonds are hiding between the pages," he said, and took up the plastic bottle of aspirin. "Now this is more like it!" He shook the bottle, imagining he was hearing the rattle of diamonds. He poured the pills onto the paperback. "Curses, foiled again."

When everything had been subjected to a thorough scrutiny, he put it all back in the purse and sighed. "Did the T-shirt you were wearing yesterday have any pockets?" he asked hopefully.

"Nope. And no diamonds fell out of my shoes when I took them off, either. Maybe he threw them out the bus window. That's why you asked me if it was open!" she exclaimed.

"And that's why I was late for dinner. I scurried back to customs and sifted the sand, unsuccessfully. I also searched the bus."

"What were you doing when you weren't at the registry office yesterday afternoon?" she asked.

"Searching the bus with Gloria, and helping her braid her hair, so it'd look as if she'd been to a hairdresser."

The image this called up lent a sharp edge to Dawn's thoughts, but she quelled it. "You're really thorough," she complimented.

"I am thoroughly confused," he admitted. "I don't suppose he could have swallowed them?"

"He took some pills!" Dawn said excitedly. "Two little pink ones. A diuretic, I think he called them."

"The diamonds weren't pink, and we searched his pill bottles. They seemed like such an obvious place. Hofstetter would never be obvious. Gloria was keeping a very close eye on him. She's certain he didn't manage to get them into anyone's pocket when everyone got off the bus."

Dawn tried to remember those moments, but Hofstetter had been behind her. "Just after Mac announced that we had to get off the bus, Hofstetter asked me about my work. He asked if our catering business was done at home, and I told him we had a separate place now, on the main street. He even asked the name. That *does* sound as though he had planted the diamonds on me, and he wanted to know where to recover them, doesn't it?"

Nick looked interested. "It sure does. We're on the right track. We just have to keep thinking." He felt uneasy, realizing that this defenseless woman was the target of Werfel's ruthless gang. He didn't want to frighten her, but he did want her to be careful. "You realize he won't stop till he finds them," he said, and gave her a warning look.

His meaning seeped in slowly. Dawn swallowed and said in a small voice, "You mean they might—kill me?"

He grabbed her hands. "I don't think they'd go that far, but they've already coshed you once. Did he hit very hard?"

"Feel the bump," she said, and bent her head.

Nick put his fingers in the silken tousled curls and gently pressed the swelling. He felt as guilty as if he'd hit her himself. "That must have hurt like hell." It was a high bump, but not big. The kind of bump the butt of a gun would make. Dawn was in danger, and it was partially his fault. The decent thing to do would be to get her out of here. Into a hospital, maybe or spirited off, away from this tour.

"It didn't hurt as much as I thought it would. I guess I have a hard head," she joked.

"Hard, but not unbreakable. Have you given any thought at all to leaving the tour, Dawn? It might be safer for you." He said it reluctantly. Some selfish corner of his mind didn't want her to go.

"Are you trying to get me killed?" she asked. "I'm the one they're after. If I left, I'd be alone. I'm safer in the middle of the group, with you and Gloria and everybody to help me. And even if I went home—well, Hofstetter *did* ask where I worked. He'd just send his man after me."

This was true, and Nick decided he could enjoy Dawn's company without feeling he was being self-

ish. "Wise as well as brave—and beautiful," he said
with an admiring smile.

Dawn felt a warm glow inside, and had to remind
herself that Nick would never be interested in a cook,
which was what she was really. She rolled her eyes up
in mockery. "You don't have to pretend you like me
any longer, Nick."

"Pretend? What do you think I am?" he demanded, insulted.

"I think you're a nice man trying to recover his
property," she said calmly. He hadn't taken advantage of her last night. He had realized she was inexperienced, and his basic integrity had held him back—
at least till she'd goaded him. She no longer thought
it was a good idea to goad Nick Barnaby. "It looks like
I'm involved whether I want to be or not, so let's just
get on with it."

"But I *do* like you," he said, with enough heat that
she felt he meant it.

"Good. I like you, too. Now, if Hofstetter somehow got word to his colleague about what he did with
the diamonds, and if I've got them without knowing
it, I think I just figured out why that man took my
hotel key. He's planning to get into my room and recover them." She jumped up and made a strangled
sound. "Nick, he's probably doing it now! While
we're here talking."

"But you've cleared out your room," he reminded
her. "Your luggage is safe behind the desk."

"Oh, right. I nearly had a heart attack. Well then,
we'd better go back to the hotel and tell them I want
my old room back. I hope he hasn't searched it already. He'll probably lie low for a while, since he must
know I'd report the attack. Anyone would. He prob-

ably plans to sneak in late at night, when I'm sleeping."

This conjured up a horrifying picture for Nick. "No! We're not using you for bait!" he said firmly.

"I'm not a complete dope. I didn't intend to crawl into bed and go to sleep, you know. I thought you could set a trap. You and the house detective could be waiting for him."

Nick looked interested in this idea. "Gloria might go for that," he said.

Dawn was aware of a hot spurt of anger, or perhaps jealousy. She didn't want beautiful, glamorous Gloria Barker infringing on her case. "She can't say no if we don't tell her," she suggested with a tempting smile. "With you and Mr. Francis, we don't need her."

"She's a trained agent, Dawn. We have to tell her." Nick noticed Dawn's pouting expression. She didn't like that. Dawn might talk about getting on with the case, but he suspected that she was enjoying his company a little. He would have preferred to keep Gloria out of it, too, but with Dawn's safety at stake, that idea was unthinkable. There'd be plenty of time to get to know her better after he recovered his diamonds. He'd give her the royal treatment in Toronto, to repay her.

"I suppose so," she agreed. "Shall we go?"

They drove back to Kingston. Nick took Mac's advice and parked in the hotel garage. At the desk, Dawn inquired if anyone had been put into room 328 yet.

"No, but the other room had been vacated now, Miss Roberts. Do you want to go up?" the clerk asked.

"I'd like my old room back, please," she said.

"But your key was taken! It might not be safe."

She saw the man was going to give her a hard time. "I found the key," she said, aware of Nick's surprise and approval. He hadn't thought she was quick enough to come up with that. She was determined to show him she was just as smart as Gloria Barker, even if she wasn't a trained agent.

"Oh, I'm glad," the clerk said. "We were all worried about you, Miss Roberts."

Nick knew that could be just hotel courtesy, but the man sounded sincere. There was something about Dawn that got through a person's veneer of sophistication and cynicism. What was it about her—her youthful innocence? That trick she had just played on the clerk didn't seem much like childish innocence. She was clever—and darned cute.

The clerk went to get her luggage, and Nick said in a low voice, "How are we going to get in? You don't have a key."

She looked at the hook behind the counter, where the other key hung. "He seems to have gone into an office. I'll risk it," she whispered.

Nick watched in disbelief as she walked unconcernedly behind the counter and took the key. The clerk came back while she was there. "Is something the matter, Miss Roberts?" he asked. "You really shouldn't be—"

She gave the man an innocent smile. "I just wanted to see what it was like back here, where you work."

Another customer approached the desk. The clerk said "I'm busy right now, but if you're really interested, I could call you after work," he suggested hopefully.

"Our group is going to be at the cabaret tonight. Why don't you come?" she asked with a flirtatious smile. Then she took her suitcase and joined Nick.

She saw the laughter in his eyes when he spotted the key dangling from her fingers. "Porter, ma'am?" he asked, and took the bag.

They walked to the elevator. "It's that innocent look you wear," he decided. "That's what it is. Nobody looks for tricks from you—poor souls. Little do they know they're dealing with Baby-face Roberts."

"The lightest fingers in the west," she said, smiling, and jingled the key from its metal tag. "We have to notify Mr. Francis and set up the trap."

Nick didn't mention Gloria. He'd have to tell her, but with luck, she'd be following up some other aspect of the case. "Let's submit your luggage to a good search first. You might have put something from your purse into your suitcase without thinking. I only had a quick look before."

"All right, but be sure you put the chain on the door. Remember, my attacker has a key, too."

"We'll change rooms," Nick decided. "You take mine; we'll do our search there, and I'll move my stuff to your room."

Dawn scowled. "You're just trying to shoehorn me out of the case," she accused him.

"I'm trying to keep your head in one piece. Besides, I have a gun."

This lent a whole new feeling of menace to the case. A gun was so—serious. "You do?"

"I often carry valuables when I travel. I have a permit for it."

They went to Nick's room and opened the case on the bed. Dawn suddenly felt shy, revealing her intimate apparel to Nick's gaze. She hastily pulled her lingerie to one side. "I'll search these," she said, and turned her back to hide the little pile from him.

"Spoilsport." He laughed. "I've already seen them."

In the mirror he saw the flush of pink under her freckles, and a smile twitched his lips. He watched as she shook out panties and bras. They were all white, unadorned. Yes, that was the kind of woman she was. Modest, practical. She bought for comfort and convenience, not to impress anyone. He picked up a garment from the suitcase and looked at it. It was a filmy black nightie with a lace inset at the bodice.

"What have we here!" he exclaimed in surprise.

Dawn looked over her shoulder and snatched it angrily from him. "What does it look like?" she asked sharply.

"It looks like a very sexy nightie. I'm shocked at you, Dawn. A woman doesn't wear black lace to impress herself."

"It was a gift," she said swiftly. It was a present to herself, bought for the trip, so she wasn't exactly telling a lie. She knew when she bought it that it was foolish, but some secret corner of her heart had harbored unrealistic ideas of encountering romance along the way.

He felt a sting at her explanation. No one but a man would buy a black lace nightie for a woman. It suggested the sort of life he thought her innocent of. "I imagine the donor planned to have the pleasure of seeing it on you," he said.

"Imagine what you like, but don't hold me responsible for your crazy ideas." She tossed the nightie aside.

What Nick found himself imagining was Dawn, dressed in that diaphanous gown. It was a disturbing image. "I suppose you have a boyfriend back home," he said, trying to hide his anger.

She replied unconcernedly, "Lots of them."

"Anyone in particular?" he persisted.

She turned and stared him in the eye. "I bought it as a present for myself. Is that what you want to know? I don't know what business it is of yours," she added.

He reached out and touched her cheek. "None of my business, except that you nearly shattered one of my most cherished ideals," he said softly. The words came out spontaneously, involuntarily. He didn't quite know what he meant himself, except that Dawn seemed like that obsolete thing—a modest, unspoiled woman who wasn't a bore. In fact, he was beginning to find her a little too fascinating. And he had been upset to think he might be wrong about the modesty.

"What have you got against black lace?" she asked, but didn't wait for an answer. "It seems to me it goes pretty well with diamonds." She pulled out a sundress and felt in the pocket, though she knew it was empty.

Nick let the subject drop. He took out a pair of sneakers and shook them. "Are these your baseball shoes?" he asked.

"No, I have special shoes for baseball. Those are walking sneakers."

Dawn hung up her three dresses, since she would be staying in this room. Soon the case was empty, their job done.

"Let's take your luggage to 328 and have a look around, see if the man has been in there, searching," she suggested.

"A good idea."

Nick gathered up his belongings and they went across the hall. The room didn't seem to have been disturbed. "Time to call Mr. Francis," he said, and picked up the phone.

The house detective arrived in five minutes. Despite the air-conditioning in the hotel, he looked hot, maybe because he was about twenty pounds overweight. "What's up, folks?" he asked. "Any news on the suspect? I'm surprised to find you're still on this floor, Miss Roberts. I understood you changed rooms. You really shouldn't come back here. We wouldn't want anything to happen to you."

There it was again, Nick noticed. That concern for Dawn. "We just switched with each other," he said. "I'm going to tell you something that I don't want to get around, Mr. Francis."

The man lounged against the wall. "If it's about Werfel, Miss Barker already told me. I'm an ex-cop. She checked me out, and decided she could trust me. And by the way, my friends call me Frank. My parents had no originality. They called me Francis Francis. So what's up, Mr. Barnaby?"

"Nick, please," he said, and outlined Dawn's plan.

Frank nodded. "It might work. We'll do a stakeout tonight. It'll look less suspicious if Miss Roberts does the usual tour business. Bloucher has already searched her bag, so she should be safe, but we'll have Miss Barker keep an eye on her."

"Is Bloucher the man who attacked me?" Dawn asked.

"That's what Miss Barker tells me. She ran a make on him, and from the description Nick gave us, it sounds like him. She's out looking for him now. She figures one of the smaller, cheaper hotels. We should clear this plan with her, eh, Nick?"

Nick looked at Dawn, "Yes, I'll speak to her," he said.

Dawn couldn't object, when the whole matter was becoming so official. "Is there anything we can do now?" she asked.

"Just do whatever you'd do if you'd never heard of Werfel," Frank suggested. "Act as if you knew nothing."

"I guess that means I go for a swim," Dawn decided.

"You'll be accompanying Miss Roberts?" Frank asked Nick.

Nick looked at Dawn with a glow of pleasure. "That's what I'd be doing if I'd never heard of Werfel," he said.

Dawn felt a thrill of happiness at his words, and the way he said them. He seemed to be saying he enjoyed her company, that it wasn't just the case of the stolen diamonds that had drawn him to her. "I'll go and change," she said.

"I'll guard the door while you do it," Frank added.

Dawn felt secure, knowing a husky man was outside her door. She changed into her bathing suit and wore her terry-cloth beach robe for the trip down on the elevator. Just before she left, she put on more sunscreen. It was a scorcher of a day, and the pool was an outdoor one.

When she came out, Frank had left, and it was Nick who was standing guard, already dressed in his bathing trunks. The dark eyes examining her held a secret warmth. "It ain't black lace, but it ain't bad," he said with a grin.

Dawn tossed her head, pretending she wasn't thrilled to death at the compliment, and wished she had brought a more daring bathing suit.

Chapter Seven

When Nick and Dawn reached the pool, they found the tour group enjoying a swim. Once the group ascertained that Dawn had recovered from her blow on the head, they subjected her to some good-natured teasing about her afternoon off with Nick.

"We won't ask what you were doing." Herb grinned in an insinuating way.

"We just went for a drive," Dawn said.

"Sure. Did you get beyond the parking lot?"

"We certainly did," she said angrily. "Just what are you implying, Herb?"

"Hey, take it easy," he said. "We're all adults, right?"

"Right." Nick smiled ironically. "But some of us are more adult than others."

"Boy, talk about no sense of humor," Herb said grouchily and left them.

Nick turned to Dawn. "Does it bother you so much that he thinks we're ... friends?" he asked.

"He doesn't think we're friends. He thinks we're lovers," she snapped. "And I do mind."

"It's not a bad idea to let him think so. It'll explain our spending a lot of time together the next day or so."

Dawn had mixed feelings about spending a lot of time with Nick, but before she could sort out her feelings, Gloria came out to the pool and everyone's attention was diverted to her. Her tanned, graceful body showed to advantage in a skimpy white bikini. With her mane of silky blond hair, she looked like a movie star. The eyes of every adult at the pool, both men and women, followed her movements as she swayed toward Nick's table. Dawn suddenly felt about as attractive as a wet cat.

"May I?" Gloria asked, and sat down at their table without waiting for an answer. "How are you feeling, Dawn?"

"Fine, thanks," Dawn replied, and attempted a smile.

"I decided to skip the tour this afternoon and spent the afternoon exploring the city," Gloria said. She gave Nick a long look as she spoke.

Now that Dawn was aware of why Gloria was here, she realized that what looked like a seductive gaze was actually something else. Gloria was really saying, we have to talk about the case.

"Any sign of Bloucher?" Nick asked.

Gloria gave him a quelling look. "I beg your pardon?"

"Dawn knows," he said.

"This is supposed to be a secret!" Gloria said sharply.

"Dawn's involved. It's obvious she's the one Bloucher is after," Nick said firmly. "You told me she wasn't in any danger. It's pretty clear she is, so I told her."

"He wouldn't have hurt her," Gloria said.

"Try telling my head that," Dawn retorted. Gloria glanced at her, with an expression that might have been meant for an apology.

"You had already searched Dawn's purse in Gananoque, so I knew Bloucher wouldn't find anything," Gloria said to Nick. "I didn't want to show our hand by following him when he followed her."

Dawn didn't enjoy being discussed as if she weren't there, and included herself in the conversation. "Did you manage to find out where he's staying? Frank said you were looking for him."

"He's not at any of the hotels," Gloria said. "I tried a dozen or so of the private homes that rent rooms to tourists as well. No luck there, either. Of course he may not have checked in anywhere yet. He won't leave town till we do. We'll just have to sit tight and let him come to us."

"We think he may do it tonight," Nick said, and outlined their plan.

Gloria didn't even try to hide her annoyance. "I'm in charge of this case, Nick," she said. "However, since he got Dawn's key, he might try to get into her room. And since you've already set it up with Francis, I'll go along with it. We'll take turns on the stakeout. We should both make an appearance at whatever the tour has planned for tonight, as well. Bloucher knows Werfel has been taken into custody, so the tour cover is blown. He'll expect that we're on the lookout. He just doesn't know which individuals he's dealing with. He'll certainly check to see that Dawn is with the group before he goes to her room. It's imperative that she stays in plain view downstairs all evening."

Dawn would have preferred to do the stakeout with Nick, but she realized that Gloria was right. Bloucher would check to see she was out of her room before he went in.

"I'll have a word with Francis now," Gloria continued. "We'll have to arrange some electronic communication so we can notify the others when he makes his attempt. If we're lucky, he'll do it during dinner, and we'll have this over with early. God, I hope so. A Pennypinchers' tour isn't exactly my idea of high living. Or yours, either, I imagine," she added with a teasing look at Nick.

Dawn felt as if they were laughing at her. She knew Gloria didn't mean it that way. It was just a thoughtless comment, but it drew attention to the difference between Dawn's social status and Nick's. Dawn glanced at him, and found him studying her.

Then he looked at Gloria. "To tell the truth, I've been having a marvelous time." Gloria clearly took the statement as a compliment to herself and she gave him a big smile before she left.

In a disgruntled mood, Dawn said, "You haven't been having the Pennypinchers' tour, Nick. You haven't even been on the bus yet, except to search it."

"But I've met some interesting people," he countered. The light in his eyes told her which one in particular he meant. "And now I'm going to enjoy the pool that our economy tour provides. Can I trust you not to get yourself kidnapped if I have a quick dip?"

"Go ahead. He's not likely to try anything at a crowded pool, and you can be sure I won't wander off again."

Nick stood up and gazed down at her. "I consider that a promise."

She watched as he walked to the deep end. Sunshine highlighted the muscles of his wide shoulders as he moved, painting them a shimmering bronze. White bathing trunks rode low on his hips, accentuating his tapered waist. He had a perfect build. He was incredibly handsome, rich, and he had a sense of humor. He was the perfect man, and she only regretted that she couldn't be a perfect woman to match him. She had saved for months for this economy tour. It was the highlight of her holidays, and to Nick it was just an inconvenience.

She watched the perfect man perform a perfect dive into the pool, wondering what sort of holidays he usually took. Nick had told her they had clients in Europe, and obviously he or someone from Verely had to meet with those clients. He'd be familiar with all the world capitals: Paris, London, Rome.

Dawn had always wanted to go to France. She'd been studying French for two years. She'd step up her saving rate as soon as she got home, and next year she'd go to Paris. She'd see all the famous places, the Louvre and the Eiffel Tower. She'd walk down the Champs Elysées. Maybe she'd see Nick.... So that was what her subconscious was up to. She smiled ruefully at her folly. By next year, he probably wouldn't even recognize her.

Nick was soon back, urging her to have a swim. "The water's fine."

"I was just waiting for you to come and guard my purse," she said. "A swim in a pool is a real luxury for me," she added. There was no point trying to pretend she was anything but what she was. A woman of modest means, who had to work hard for her living.

He reached out and tousled her curls. "To see you in a bathing suit is a luxury for all of us," he joked.

She noticed with satisfaction that a few heads did turn as she went to the edge of the pool. There were so many people swimming that it wasn't very much fun, and she didn't stay in long. When she went back to the table, she found Nick had ordered drinks, and the two of them sat beneath the umbrella, talking.

"What's on for tonight?" Nick asked.

"There's a cabaret here at the hotel. The Flamingo Room has live entertainment and dancing. We had a choice of that or summer theater. I'd already seen *The Glass Menagerie*, so I opted for the cabaret."

"Good choice. Tennessee Williams would be a little hard on the seat of the pants in weather like this."

"Do you go to the theater much, Nick?" she asked. This was her chance to learn something about his private life, his likes and dislikes.

"When I get the chance, I do. London has the best live theater at the moment, I think. Of course Broadway's pretty good, too. Actually I prefer the opera. I saw Pavarotti at La Scala last month."

He had mentioned London, New York and Italy in one answer. He was obviously a true cosmopolitan, which only added to her insecurity. "I've never been to Rome," she said wistfully.

"A lot of people think La Scala's in Venice or Rome. Actually it's in Milan," he said, not in a putting-down way, but just making a comment.

He didn't seem to be astonished at her ignorance, but Dawn felt a rush of embarrassment. To make a joke of it she said, "I must have been thinking of the Grand Canal. Of course that's in Rome."

"That and the Eiffel Tower." He grinned. "Right next door to the Louvre. Have you been to Europe yet?"

Yet. How thoughtful of him to put it that way, as if it were a mere oversight on her part. "Not yet," she said.

"You've been too busy making those shrimp puffs, huh? There's plenty of time. You're young."

"I'm twenty-two," she pointed out swiftly.

Nick realized he had unintentionally stepped on her toes. "I don't know why you're so eager to be old. It's wonderful to be young. You have the whole world to discover. All the best things are still before you. Your first view of Paris from the top of the Eiffel Tower, a gondola ride by moonlight down the Grand Canal, the buskers and pearlies in London, an eel pie in a British pub." He wanted to show her those things, to relive the excitement of his early youth through her eager eyes. At times, Nick felt jaded. Europe was like his second home. Those long transatlantic trips had become more of a nuisance than anything else.

"Eel pie!" she said, wrinkling her nose. "It sounds awful."

"And you call yourself a gourmet!" he scoffed in a bantering way. "I bet you've never had bubble and squeak, either, or my own favorite, bangers and mash."

"I've often had bangers and mash," she objected. "We call it sausages and mashed potatoes. It's pretty gross, too."

"That'd be because you didn't have warm ale with it. They serve ale warm in England. That's one of their treats I could do without."

"What's your favorite country?" she asked, eager to learn more about him. That comment about bangers and mash told her he didn't limit himself to the high life.

For the next minutes, Nick talked about Paris and London, and Dawn listened, entranced. She could almost imagine she was there, on the banks of the Seine, when he described the lime trees and chestnut trees in spring. He noticed the little things, as well as the big tourist attractions. Finally Nick suggested another beer—cold beer—and when they looked around for a waiter, they were surprised to see that nearly everyone had left.

"How time flies when you're having fun," Nick said. It had been fun, talking to Dawn, getting to know her a little, discovering she was exactly the kind of nice, innocent person he had thought. Yet not lacking maturity and intelligence. She hadn't traveled, but she read, and dreamed. He thought of that incongruous black lace nightie in her suitcase.

"We'd better go and change for dinner," she said, and began gathering up her purse and coat.

Their conversation had made Dawn hungry for romance. Thinking about Europe always made her feel that way. But at least this evening she would have the excitement of the cabaret, with music and dancing—and Nick. She wore her most becoming outfit, a blue sundress with spaghetti straps and a full skirt. She would have loved white, but it didn't suit her pale coloring. Since she had to avoid the sun, there was no dramatic contrast of the sort Gloria's tan provided.

She had to provide her own drama by wearing big, dangling earrings and a deep blue shawl shot with gold threads. The canvas bag was definitely out of place. She put her essentials into a smaller white evening bag and went out the door. Nick was waiting for her, looking up and down the hall.

He studied her with approval. "You look *magnifique*! I wish I could bundle you on to a jet and fly you off to Paris," he said, taking her arm.

"I wish you could, too," she said with enthusiasm.

Nick looked at her with rising interest. No reason he couldn't, when this affair was settled. "Do you have a passport?" he asked.

She blinked in surprise. He wasn't kidding! Nick Barnaby really lived in the fast lane. Much too fast for her, and she'd better squelch that idea fast, before she succumbed to temptation. "No, but I *do* have a mother who would agree with me that flying off to Europe with a man I hardly know was just a little abrupt."

"Ah yes, mothers. I have one of those myself. Mine has a passport," he added thoughtfully. And she loved Paris, if Dawn required a chaperon. It really would be fun to show Dawn the sights.

Dawn didn't know what he meant by that last statement, unless he was hinting that his mother was known to have an occasional fling herself. She was a widow, so maybe that was it. Best to change the subject. "No sign of Bloucher having been in your room?" she asked.

"No. Frank has alerted the staff and given them Bloucher's description. They only know that he's a possible thief. If anyone sees him, they report to Frank. Our orders are to behave as though we haven't a care in the world. That means we get to enjoy dinner and the dance."

"I can live with that," she said, smiling.

The group had a reserved table in the main dining room. There were only two choices for dinner, steak or chicken supreme. Dawn chose the steak. One of her mother's dishes was chicken supreme, and she had it often. The other people at the table were all talking about the afternoon tour. Miss Edmonds asked a few questions about why Nick hadn't gone, when it would have given him such good background for his thesis.

"I plan to make a long stop here after the tour," Nick said. "One day is hardly worth the effort, so I took Dawn for a drive instead, to help her recuperate."

Miss Edmonds examined the younger woman with a laughing eye and said, "It worked."

Nick inclined his head to Dawn and said in a low voice, "I never told so many lies in my life. My nose hasn't grown a foot or so, has it?"

At the other end of the table, Gloria flirted with Herb, looking as if she were carefree. What a good actress she is, Dawn thought. She's probably despising every minute of this, but you'd never guess it from her behavior. The only crack in her veneer was those long looks she passed down the table to Nick. Dawn didn't think they were all about business. She didn't think Gloria would refuse a quick flight to Paris, either, if Nick asked her. Obviously she was the kind of woman he was used to—sophisticated, glamorous, passport at the ready to fly off into the wild blue yonder at the drop of a hat. Gloria had probably been to La Scala dozens of times.

In the after-dinner confusion, Gloria worked her way toward Nick and Dawn. She handed Nick a little black box. "Stick this in your pocket. It's a transmitter and receiver. It'll give a little bleep if Francis wants to speak to you, so you'd better have an excuse ready, in case anyone hears it. You could always say it's an electronic timer to remind you to make a phone call. That's what I plan to say."

She showed Nick how to operate the gizmo. "Do I get one?" Dawn asked.

"You don't need one, Dawn. This is to call us upstairs if Bloucher comes," Gloria said. "You're to stay down here, and don't wander off by yourself. It's safer that way."

"I'll stay with Dawn till it's my turn to guard the room," Nick said.

"I'll spell Francis in an hour. See you." Gloria waggled her fingers and left.

Before they went to the cabaret, Nick and Dawn strolled down to the water. In July, the evenings were long, and the sun was just sinking into the horizon, turning the water to crimson. A cool breeze blew in, rippling the surface.

"This is so beautiful, I don't know why we think we have to go to Europe to see the sights," Nick said.

"It's another whole world over there, the Old World. It's not so much the scenic wonders as the architecture and art that interest me. And of course the people."

Nick studied her closely. The last rays of the sun were vanishing. He watched, enchanted, as the rosy glow reflecting on Dawn's face faded to the shadows of evening. "There's nothing wrong with the people here," he said in a husky voice. It seemed the perfect moment for a kiss. He wanted to taste her lips leisurely, and not with the stupid sort of attack he'd made in anger the night before.

But there were others out enjoying the sunset, and he was coming to know Dawn well enough to realize she wouldn't like a public display of affection. His pride wouldn't enjoy a public rebuff, either. He took her hand and said, "It's not a good idea for me to keep you out after dark when we know Bloucher's hanging around. Let's go in."

The musicians in the Flamingo Room were just tuning up their instruments. A big neon flamingo glowed on the wall above them. Potted palms lent an exotic touch to the room.

"We'll do what travelers do in dangerous foreign ports, and sit with our back to the wall, watching the door," Nick said, using his words as an excuse to lead her to a dark corner, where they could enjoy privacy.

"Do you travel to dangerous ports in your business?" she asked, hoping to hear some stories of intrigue.

"You mean places like Macao and Hong Kong, where life is cheap and they stick a knife between your ribs and steal your diamonds as quick as they can blink?" Nick teased. "No, actually we buy most of our gems in London. I learned these survival tactics from old movies."

"I love old movies," Dawn said, surprised to find they had a taste in common. "I've seen *Casablanca* six times."

"Only six?" he asked, grinning. "I must have seen it a dozen. Of course by the time you reach my age, you'll probably have seen it more often."

"For sure! And *The Maltese Falcon*! I love that one."

"You don't fool me. What *you* love is Humphrey Bogart. He's a tough act to follow. Shall we ask Sam to play our song?"

"Play it again, you mean," she said.

It was a wonderful evening. In that exotic-seeming spot, with the thrill of imminent danger all about them, they pretended they were at Rick's place. They picked out their cast of characters from the people at nearby tables, and didn't forget to keep watch for the real criminal as well. Dawn would only let Nick have one drink, and smiled to see the dashing Nick Barnaby order a Shirley Temple when the waiter came for the second time. "Make it a double," he added incongruously. The waiter frowned. "Two cherries," Nick said.

"You're crazy," she charged.

He grabbed her fingers and said with his best Humphrey Bogart impersonation, "I'm crazy about you, kid. Of all the economy tours in all the countries, you had to pick mine."

"Actually you picked mine."

"Same difference. If it weren't for the Fat Man— that's Werfel—we never would have met."

"Wrong movie, Nick. That was *The Maltese Falcon*."

"Wrong bird, too," he said, glancing at the red flamingo. Then he turned back to her. "But the right woman, as far as I'm concerned."

They danced and talked and joked. Later, Gloria came down and said, "All's quiet above. Your turn, Nick."

The evening was much less enjoyable once Nick left for the stakeout. Dawn had a few dances with the desk clerk she had invited to meet her. She danced with other men, too, but she didn't talk much. In her mind, she was still with Nick, having the most enjoyable evening of her life, and wishing it could go on forever. Nick was on duty from ten to eleven. When he came down, Frank had replaced him, and there was still no sign of Bloucher.

"He's had hours to get in," Gloria said. "I wonder if he's going to make his move at all. Maybe he'll wait till we get to Toronto."

"Maybe—" Nick paused, frowning. "Maybe he isn't coming. Stay with Dawn, Gloria. I just had an idea." He hurried out of the cabaret and went to the front desk to borrow a flashlight.

In ten minutes, he was back. "He isn't coming," he said, and handed Dawn her room key.

"This isn't mine. Mine is in my purse," she said.

"This is the one you lost this morning. It just occured to me that he might not have your key at all, and he doesn't. This was hanging from a branch in that bush where he tossed your purse. In the confusion of your attack this morning, we didn't search very carefully, and missed this."

"Oh damn! A whole night wasted," Gloria exclaimed. "He must have seen the key. Why didn't he take it?"

Nick wrinkled his brow. "Maybe because he doesn't think the diamonds are in Dawn's room. The thing is, he knows where they are, and we don't. I'm assuming Hofstetter told him. He thought they were in Dawn's bag. You said nothing was missing, right?"

"Nothing was missing," she agreed.

"We practically tore that purse apart," Nick said to Gloria.

Gloria just looked bewildered. "I just don't understand. Did you check your clothes, Dawn?"

"Every stitch. I was only wearing shorts and a shirt. Maybe the man who attacked me has nothing to do with Hofstetter."

Gloria shook her head. "No, that would be too much coincidence. The description Nick gave me matches Bloucher exactly. He's a known member of Werfel's gang. And he didn't steal your wallet, so he isn't just an ordinary purse snatcher. If you're sure he didn't take anything from your purse, then he didn't get the diamonds. We'll just have to wait for him to come back. He'll probably wait a few days. I figure he'll hit in Toronto. The Werfel gang prefer large cities. It's easier to move around unnoticed. I'm going to call it a night."

"Let's all call it a night," Dawn said.

"Will you be staying with Dawn?" Gloria asked Nick.

Dawn gave her a freezing stare. "Of course he won't be staying with me!"

"For protection," Gloria added, surprised.

Dawn felt foolish, rushing in to preserve her reputation when it hadn't been under attack. All she had done was show them both what was on her mind. "I don't need protection," she said, "I've changed rooms with Nick, and anyway Bloucher doesn't even have the key."

Gloria shrugged. "Suit yourself." Then she gave a worldly laugh. "Personally, I think it makes a great excuse." Then she finally left.

"What do you say?" Nick asked. "I promise to behave, if that's what worries you. It isn't a bad idea, you know. He just might find out we changed rooms."

"I don't see how he could. No one in the hotel even knows we switched rooms. No, I'm sure it isn't necessary. I'll lock my door and put on the chain."

"If you hear anything in the night, just holler. I'll be right across the hall, and I'm a light sleeper." He didn't plan to sleep at all, unless he could get Frank to spell him in watching Dawn's door—just in case.

They went up on the elevator together and he walked Dawn to her room. He went in with her, just to make sure Bloucher hadn't found out about the room change and paid a call. Nothing had been disturbed.

"I guess everything is all right," Nick said. "You can slip into that sexy, black lace nightie and get a good night's sleep." He could just picture her in it. It had a plunging neckline, and the lace made the top translucent. Her creamy skin would show through. When he took her in his arms, the material would be cool and slinky to the touch, but with warm, firm, feminine flesh beneath. Those curves he'd admired when she wore her bathing suit would move beneath his touch. He could almost feel her.

Dawn noticed Nick's change of mood. His mouth relaxed, and a sultry heat came from his eyes, which were exploring her minutely. She felt an answering heat as the sexual tension grew. "I'll say good-night then," she said, but her voice was uneven.

"Kiss good-night, you mean?" he asked, taking her hands and pulling her toward him.

After their shared adventure, a good-night kiss seemed natural. Dawn didn't want to appear prudish, but she was afraid that in this mood, one kiss would be one too many. She hesitated, and he pulled her into his arms. His lips touched her gently, so differently from last night.

Nick wanted to make up for their kiss yesterday. He could see she was uncertain, and he wanted to allay her fears. His arms closed around her slowly, leaving time for her to withdraw. He felt her tremble for a moment, and was afraid she was going to push him away. He just clung to her lips, without increasing the pressure, till he felt her arms circle his neck. They felt tentative, like the brush of a bird's wing. He held her more closely, till he could feel the thrust of her breasts against his chest, engrossingly intimate, disturbingly alluring, totally feminine. An ache of desire flamed.

As their bodies touched, his lips firmed and he crushed her against him in a real kiss. Nick was no puritan. He had made love to women in many countries, practiced, experienced beautiful women, but he had never felt this surge of tender, protective emotion. And it wasn't just his fear of what Bloucher might do that caused it, either. He wanted to protect her from the world, maybe even from himself. Something inside him seemed to grow and swell, and consume him with a physical need, but it was a need he was willing to fight. He had never thought so much more of his partner's pleasure than his own, but it was of Dawn that he thought now. Take it easy, go slow or you'll frighten her to death.

After the first light embrace, Dawn was lost to her emotions. She was caught up in a hazy, heady thrill of discovery. Her eyes flickered open, just once, to make sure she wasn't dreaming. It really was Nick Barnaby, the perfect man, and not a dream. His lips bruised hers in a soul-destroying kiss. She felt the flick of his tongue, and eased her mouth open. It was a dreadful mistake. He was inside her, claiming her with masterful strokes that left her weak. An inchoate moan echoed from deep within her.

The low sound brought her back to reality, and she gently pulled away. "Well, we've said good-night, kissed good-night. There's nothing left to...say." Her voice was uneven, breathless.

Nick looped his arms around her waist and studied her. She looked drugged. "I can think of several things to say—and do," he said huskily. "Both you and your mother would hate every one of them, so I'll leave. Sleep tight." He placed a kiss on her forehead and left.

When the door closed, Dawn said quietly, "That's what you think!"

Chapter Eight

Dawn realized she was out of her league with Nick, and knew she should cut off the affair before she got hurt. She didn't think he would hurt her intentionally—it wasn't his fault that she'd lain awake for hours, reliving that kiss. It was just that he moved in the fast lane; he was a jet-setter, while she drove the company van. If they stayed together for the whole week, she'd be so much in love with him she'd be a basket case. And the way to bring this adventure to a close was to find the diamonds and catch Bloucher. She thought and schemed, and finally came up with something.

Nick phoned early the next morning, an hour before the tour was meeting for breakfast. The jangling of the phone woke Dawn from a sound sleep. "Hello," she said, confused.

"Good morning, sleepyhead. Did I wake you up?"

"Yes," she said, rather crossly.

"Sorry, but you don't need beauty sleep. You're beautiful enough." Nick pictured her in bed, her hair tousled, her eyes heavy. She'd be wearing that irresistible pout—and equally irresistible black lace nightie. He felt a shiver of fear, in case anything should happen to her. Good Lord, was he falling in love?

"What do you want?" she asked.

"You'd split my head open if I told you," he said in a soft voice. "And besides, what I want can't be accomplished over the phone. I called to tell you I just had a buzz from Gloria. She suggested we go down early to talk in private. Can you get dressed in five minutes?"

Dawn shook herself fully awake. "Oh—sure, I'll be there."

"Don't leave your room alone. I'll meet you in the hall."

She scrambled out of bed and got dressed quickly. Nick tapped at her door a few minutes later, and she invited him into her room. There were dark smudges under his eyes from a sleepless night. Frank Francis had gone off duty, and his replacement had been less than helpful. Nick had had to stay awake all night himself, and he felt like a dishrag. Dawn, he noticed, was as bright and shiny as a spring day.

"I have an idea," she said. "You probably won't go for it, but it makes sense to me."

He hunched his shoulders. "Try me. If you can't convince me, no one can."

"All right, here it is. Gloria said last night that Werfel's gang likes a big city because it's easier to hide, and get away. So why give him that advantage? Why not stay away from the big city? When the tour leaves, we stay here in Kingston, or go back to an even smaller place like Gananoque. He wouldn't be hard to spot at Rockwood Manor, for instance. We could force him into the open."

"It makes sense to me," Nick said. "But I don't want to draw you into this any more deeply than you already are. You go ahead to Toronto. Gloria and I—"

Dawn objected instinctively, without even thinking out what he had said. "No. That wouldn't work. You're forgetting he thinks *I* have the diamonds," she announced triumphantly.

"Maybe we could con him into thinking that you gave them to me."

Nick and Gloria, alone in beautiful Rockwood Manor. Well, it would get her off the hook, so why not? Her head acknowledged the fact, but her heart overruled her common sense. "How would we do that? All that would happen is that he'd follow me to Toronto, and I'd be all alone, with you and Gloria hundreds of miles away."

"You could leave your big canvas purse with Gloria," he suggested.

"He's already searched it. The trouble is, we don't know where the diamonds are, but if Hofstetter told him—well, I say we lure him to some busy spot and let him come after us. We'll be ready and waiting."

Nick paced the room, worrying his lip. "I wasn't too happy with the idea of his following us to Toronto. This could just bring the whole thing to a head, but it's too dangerous. I don't want to put you at risk."

"I'm already at risk," she pointed out. "I'd be happy to have it over with, too. It's made a shambles of my holiday."

Nick felt guilty about that. He stopped pacing and put a hand on her arm. His closeness, the brush of his fingers against her flesh was an exquisite torture. "I'll make it up to you, Dawn," he promised.

She willed her tone to remain businesslike. "The best way you can do that is by catching Bloucher. I say we drop out of the tour and let him chase us till we catch him."

"You just may be right," Nick said. "We'll talk it over with Gloria."

It occurred to Dawn that Nick's convertible only held two. And she had a pretty good idea who'd fill that other seat once Gloria was involved. "You don't need her approval. You don't work for her."

"We're working *with* her," he pointed out. "Her agency has vast resources. If it weren't for them, we wouldn't even know for sure that Bloucher is part of Werfel's gang. There's a real possibility they may replace Bloucher, and we won't know who we're dealing with. But Gloria could find out."

Dawn grudgingly admitted that he was right. "We'll talk it over with her at breakfast," she said. "Let's go, before the others come down."

To make sure no early bird joined them, Nick and Dawn sat at a table for two, and got another chair when Gloria came in. "Was everything quiet last night?" she asked.

"Not a critter was stirring, not even a rat," Nick said.

"Then it's on to Toronto," Gloria said, and poured herself a cup of coffee.

"Dawn has come up with an alternative plan," Nick said, and outlined it.

Gloria looked interested. "It has possibilities," she admitted. "I imagine Bloucher or his replacement will be watching the bus when it loads up for Toronto. Probably from some concealed spot. He'll see that we don't board. What we have to do is see who follows us to your car. Oh, you forgot, Nick, your car only holds two."

"That's a good excuse for us to break up," Dawn said. "Nick and I go to the car, you hang around behind and watch to find out who's tailing us. You can use that gizmo you gave Nick last night to notify him who we should be looking out for."

"And I follow him, while he follows you," Gloria said. "Good thinking, Dawn. I'll have to hire a car."

Dawn was flattered at praise from a pro. She noticed that Gloria didn't raise any objection to losing the spot in Nick's car. Maybe her only interest in Nick *was* business.

"You realize Werfel's team is dangerous," Gloria added. "I think I'll get some backup on this. I'll give the RCMP a call. They can provide an unmarked car, and a man to come with me. It's a good idea to have a badge along anyway, to make the arrest."

"The only thing left to do then is notify Mac that we won't be continuing the tour," Dawn said.

Nick looked surprised. "That we'll be joining them in Toronto later, you mean." Dawn turned a curious look on him. Nick continuing the tour? Why?

"Speak for yourself," Gloria said. "It's back to the States for me as soon as we get this tied up. And now we'd better have a hearty breakfast. It's going to be a rough day. Order me Cream of Wheat and orange juice, will you, Nick? I'm going to make that phone call."

She left and Nick turned to Dawn. "Cream of Wheat? What does our touring gourmet think of that idea?"

"It's sensible. Cream of Wheat is very nourishing."

"I'll have the bacon and eggs," Nick said.

"Same here." She wasn't in a sensible mood.

What sat on her plate hardly mattered. Dawn found she was too upset to eat much. This game of cops and robbers might be mild stuff for Gloria, but as far as she was concerned, she was almost as scared as she was excited. Nothing like this had ever happened to her before. It was thrilling—and dangerous, and she was doing it with Nick, which added to her emotional turbulence.

After breakfast, they all went upstairs to pack and wait. In the elevator, Gloria said, "The Mountie will meet us in your room to hammer out the details, Nick. Let's all pack and meet there."

They split up and regrouped a little later. Soon a tall, blond man in a yellow shirt tapped at the door. Gloria was the closest and looked out the peephole before answering.

"Barker?" the man asked.

"Come in," she said, and closed the door behind him.

The Mountie introduced himself. He and Gloria showed each other their IDs. "John Hawthorn," he said. "I've been thinking over your plan, Miss Barker."

"You have objections?" she said stiffly.

"No, a suggestion. I'm not happy with the idea of a shoot-out in a public hotel. There's too much chance of some innocent bystander getting hurt. I suggest *we* choose the spot.''

"What do you mean?" she asked.

"There's a stretch of highway toward Gananoque where the road branches in two directions. Highway Two, which goes north, isn't used much anymore since they put in the four-lane along the river. I suggest that Mr. Barnaby take the old highway, and have a breakdown there. There's a spot with picnic tables, and a good heavy stand of pines. I can have a couple of men waiting, concealed.''

"Not a bad idea," Gloria said.

"Won't it look fishy if we pull off and stop on a quiet little road, with no scenic view to look at or anything?" Nick asked.

The Mountie gave a nervous smile. "We were discussing an idea at HQ before I left. You might not like it, Mr. Barnaby, but if the loot's worth three million, you might want to consider it.''

"Let's hear it," Nick said, curious as to what the plan could be.

"Make the breakdown look genuine. Pour some oil in your gas tank.''

Nick looked horrified. "In my new Jag?" he exclaimed. "Isn't there any other way?''

"You can just stop, and hope your man doesn't smell a trap," Hawthorn said with a noticeable lack of enthusiasm.

"You're right, of course," Nick said.

"What do you mean?" Gloria asked. "I don't get it.''

Nick frowned. "We put oil in my gas tank. It smokes—to say nothing of doing irreparable damage to my engine—and gives us an excuse to stop without making Bloucher suspect anything. In fact, it would seem the perfect time for him to attack, when the car's in trouble and we can't get away, or follow him.''

"Don't let Bloucher see you tampering with the gas tank here at the hotel," Dawn said. "We could stop at a gas station and do it."

"Good thinking," Nick said. "I need gas anyway, but I won't put in much. I don't want a whole tank mixed with oil. I might get away without destroying the engine if I only use a couple of gallons and drive a few miles."

"I'll phone HQ and have some men waiting," Hawthorn said. He outlined exactly where the rendezvous spot was. "And as an added precaution, I'll stick around the hotel and follow Bloucher. We'll have him trapped."

"I'll be working on it, too," Gloria said. "I'll keep out of sight in the lobby and join Officer Hawthorn after he spots whoever is following you. It might be Bloucher, if he thinks he got away unseen yesterday. In any case, there hasn't been much time to get another man up here. He might just wear dark glasses and a wig or something."

"I'll go on downstairs and wait," Hawthorn said. "We don't want to be seen together." He left.

"What if no one follows us?" Dawn asked.

"Then we set off after the bus and link up with the tour again at—" Gloria consulted her schedule "—a place called Port Hope. We have a coffee and comfort stop there. It's about halfway to Toronto. What'll we tell Mac? We have to let him know we aren't going on the bus."

"He must know by now that something fishy is going on," Nick said. "I'll tell him we've decided to have a look at Fort Henry after all. None of us saw it, so it might pass."

"If he doesn't happen to remember that your car only holds two," Dawn added.

Gloria looked bored. "I'm sure Herb has convinced everyone by now that I'm a loose woman. I'd really like to tell him what I think of him before he leaves. They won't have any trouble believing I stayed behind with a traveling salesman. One of the less appealing aspects of my job," she added. "Not that I care a whole lot what that crew think of me."

When they met in the lobby later, Nick put the luggage in the car, then went to speak to Mac. Dawn noticed Hawthorn reading at the rack of tourist advertisements near the front desk. He didn't look at her. Gloria went to one of the sofas in the lobby and held a newspaper in front of her face.

When Nick came back, he said, "We want to be highly visible. Let's go out and wave goodbye to them."

Dawn was reluctant to do it. "Mary Edmonds will think I've become a fallen woman," she said in a worried tone.

Nick gave her a peculiar look. "Then I'll just have to redeem your reputation," he said.

"How do you plan to do that?"

Now he was laughing. "Think about it," he advised, and took her arm to lead her out to the bus.

Instead she thought about how her leaving the tour would look to everyone. Going off alone with a man—the others would be shocked. But after Bloucher was caught, she could tell the whole story. This helped bolster her self-esteem, and she went along to wave the bus off.

"Not coming with us?" Mrs. McDougall asked. Her sharp eyes suggested that the reason couldn't possibly be a good one. "I thought this was supposed to be a family tour," she said to her husband. "We might have known what it would be like. The same with TV. The minute you turn it on, your children are subjected to something lewd. Get on the bus, girls."

Nick winked at Dawn. "Travel is so broadening," he said in a low voice.

Flora and Fiona scampered aboard, with Mrs. McDougall pushing them forward. Mr. McDougall looked apologetic. "Enjoy yourselves," he said. His harried expression said there would be little enough time for that once they were saddled with a spouse. "Oh, Miss Roberts," he added, and handed her a white bottle. "My wife says you left this at the pool yesterday. You'll want it if you plan to do any sunbathing."

"Thanks," she said, and slid her sunscreen cream into her bag.

Miss Edmonds edged forward to say goodbye. "You will be joining us tonight?" she inquired with a worried frown.

"If not tonight, then tomorrow," Dawn said.

"Oh, Dawn! Do you think this is wise, my dear?" she asked in a low voice so Nick couldn't hear.

"I'll explain everything later," Dawn promised.

"You won't do anything...rash? Mr. Barnaby is very handsome, of course, but I'm afraid he isn't the kind of man you're used to. Now don't think I'm an old nosey parker, but I'm sure if your mother were here, she'd say the same thing."

"No, she'd say much more," Dawn said. "But this really isn't what you think."

Miss Edmonds looked at her closely. "Your eyes say you're telling me the truth. I've had a lot of practice reading youngsters' faces. Whatever it is, good luck to you." Then she turned to Nick. "Take good care of her, young man. She's not one of your floozies." With this blunt speech, Miss Edmonds clambered aboard the bus.

Nick turned to Dawn. "My floozies!" he exclaimed. "She makes me sound like a sultan. Was she warning you against me?"

Dawn gave him a saucy smile. "Yes."

A smile curved his lips. "What did you say?"

"I told her not to worry. It wasn't what she thought."

"Funny, nobody seems worried about *me*. Why do they assume the man is always the villain of the piece?"

"Just common sense. It isn't a Miss Werfel who stole the diamonds, or a Miss Bloucher who stole my purse."

He grinned at her clever answer. "Or a Miss Barnaby who lured you off the bus, either."

The door closed, and the bus lumbered forward, with many people waving from the window. Fiona McDougall stuck out her tongue. "Adorable child," Nick said. "And to think, in ten or so years, some poor unsuspecting man will marry that creature."

Dawn was too nervous to banter. "Shall we go to the car now?" she asked.

"Right, without looking over your shoulder, if you can control your curiosity. It's hard not to look, isn't it?"

"Nearly impossible."

"Everyone on the bus thinks we're off on a love tryst. Shall we let Bloucher think the same thing?" he asked, and placed a light kiss on the tip of her nose. Then he took her hand and they went to the car. Nick had arranged to have it brought to the front door of the hotel. It was their chance to see if any mysterious man was watching them. The only man lingering nearby was John Hawthorn.

"Unless he's disguised as the doorman, he isn't here," Nick said.

"And if he is disguised as the doorman, he's put on about a hundred pounds since yesterday."

Nick held the door and Dawn got into the car. As they pulled out of the driveway, Nick said, "Maybe you should get the gun out. We don't want to be caught with our only defense locked up in the glove compartment."

Dawn opened the door and lifted out a little pistol. "It isn't exactly a Colt .45, is it?" she asked. It fit into the palm of her hand.

"I don't use it for shooting elephants. You can just put it on the seat between us. That'd please Miss Edmonds, if she could see it," he added.

Dawn ignored his effort to lighten the mood. "Maybe Bloucher doesn't have a car." She sounded worried.

"He was planning to follow the bus. He'll have a car." He peered into the rearview mirror. No one was following yet. "Keep your eyes peeled for a self-service gas station."

As they drove toward the eastern edge of town Dawn spotted one. "There, and it's on the right side of the road, too."

Nick pulled in. "I'll fill it while you get the oil," Dawn offered.

"It seems a desecration, like painting a mustache on the *Mona Lisa*," he said sadly when he returned with the oil, but he poured it in the tank anyway. While he paid the bill, Dawn scanned the road. No one seemed to be paying any attention to them.

Nick kept looking in the rearview mirror as they moved further out of the city. "It's smoking already," he said. "It's a good thing we only have to go three and a half miles."

"You're trying to recover three million dollars' worth of diamonds. Our lives could be at stake for all we know, and you're worrying about a stupid engine!" Dawn exclaimed.

"Stupid? It's a very clever engine. A man and his automobile are like lovers. This ain't no way to treat a lover. Although I've heard rumors of oil being used..." he added irrepressibly.

"Not engine oil, I hope," Dawn said, with a quelling look.

"I'd prefer a more delicate scent myself. Attar of roses."

"Olive oil is good," she said unthinkingly.

His head slewed around. "*Is* good?" he demanded. "Are you telling me you've—*oiled* with someone, Dawn? And here I thought you were a sweet, innocent child." She glared. "Girl." She continued glaring. "Young woman—who indulges in olive oil orgies."

"Dream on. We use it in cooking. Sometimes it spills on my hands. It's very smooth and soft, like satin."

Nick felt rather foolish at his outburst. "I suppose you've dallied innocently with whipped cream as well?" he asked playfully.

Dawn looked over her shoulder. "That smoke really smells, doesn't it?"

"I'm trying to distract myself. Tell me about you and whipped cream."

"We had a torrid romance at first. When I began to grow a spare tire, I stopped. It slowed me down when I was running."

"You're a jogger, are you?" he asked with interest. That would account for her trim body.

"I hate jogging. I told you I play baseball."

"That's very apple pie-ish and American. What position do you play?"

"Pitcher. I'm pretty good."

He flickered a glinting smile at her. "I can believe that. What's your specialty, fastball, slow ball?"

"Curveball. How much farther?"

"Two miles. Do you see any pines up ahead?"

Dawn looked out the window. "This whole highway is lined with pines. They're the most outstanding feature of the drive. Pines and the lack of traffic. The only other vehicle on the road is that old pickup truck in front of us."

"Uh-oh, fasten your safety belt," Nick said. "I've just spotted something following. He's gaining on us. If we're not careful, he'll catch us before we hit the rendezvous point." He stepped on the gas and the car sped up.

Dawn felt her stomach harden into a knot. She looked over her shoulder, but the car was only a small dot on the road. "He can't overtake us before we get there."

"I'll buzz Gloria." He took out his gizmo and began pressing the button. "I've spotted him," he said. "He's gaining on me. Have you got him in sight?"

"We didn't see anyone follow you," Gloria said. "The car behind you came out of a farm house half a mile back. It has a woman driver with a dog and a child. I think we can forget it. It's beginning to look like a bust. We'll stop at the rendezvous, though."

"You mean I wrecked my engine for nothing!"

After a short silence, Gloria spoke again. "Hawthorn says it shouldn't be wrecked in three miles," she said consolingly.

Nick pressed the button and swore. "Sorry," he said to Dawn.

"That's all right. I'd probably say the same thing if I were in your shoes. So no one followed us."

"It's on to Toronto—as soon as I get this tank drained and filled with unoiled gas."

When they spotted some rustic wooden tables and benches, they pulled over. "So this is the non-rendezvous spot," Nick said. There was no sign of anyone. He cupped his hands and shouted into the bushes. "Come out, come out, wherever you are. There's nobody here but us chickens."

The men didn't respond or appear until Hawthorn pulled in and made it official. "You can come out, boys." Two bright-eyed, uniformed young officers appeared, one from each end of the clearing. They were holding guns.

"You can put those back in your holsters," Hawthorn said.

"Now what?" Gloria asked. She was beginning to look disgruntled.

Hawthorn rubbed his jaw in consternation. "He must have been waiting on the western edge of town. I guess it didn't occur to him that you might not continue with the tour. It'll take him a while to find out."

"Before we do anything else," Nick said, "I'm getting this baby to a garage." He patted his car lovingly.

"How about me?" Gloria demanded.

"Find your own garage," Nick retorted. "Sorry, Gloria. It's not your fault. You go back to Kingston with Officer Hawthorn," he added. "We'll meet at the hotel there and continue on to—what was that place?"

"Port Hope," Dawn said. "We may be too late for that stop. If so, we'll meet the group in Toronto."

Gloria gave a deep sigh. "I'll be damned if I'm going to sit on Dawn's lap all the way to Toronto. I'll hire a car. Let's go, John."

Dawn noticed she had already achieved a first-name basis with the Mountie. The other two officers their attention evenly divided between the Jag and Gloria.

"I'll see you before you leave," Hawthorn said to Nick. "We'll set up something with the Toronto office to give you a hand. We're just as eager to catch Werfel's crew as you are, Mr. Barnaby. We have our reputation to maintain. The Mounties always get their man, you know."

"Thanks, Officer. You were very helpful."

"Sorry about the car. It should be all right. You didn't drive it far. There's no garage on this stretch of road. Not enough traffic to warrant it, but you can cut over to the highway about a mile farther along. Plenty of garages there. Shall we go, Gloria?" Hawthorn grinned at the other officers as he led Gloria off to his car.

"What should we do?" the men asked.

"Follow Mr. Barnaby and make sure he doesn't break down before he reaches a garage, then report back to HQ," Hawthorn replied.

Nick scowled and opened the door for Dawn. "I wonder if I can bill them for a new engine."

"Look on the bright side, Nick. If you break down, we get to have a ride in a cop car."

He glared at her. "Maybe they'll let us play with the siren," he said, and turned the key. The engine started up with a smooth purr and they pulled onto the road, trailing a cloud of dark smoke behind them.

Chapter Nine

There—that sign points to the Scenic Highway,''
Dawn pointed out. "It can't be much farther to a garage.''

"My poor Jag. And it's only a month old." Nick
sighed. "I should have rented a car. Why didn't I think
of that?" He turned onto the ramp. From the rear, he
heard a horn.

"Why is that Mountie blowing his horn?" Dawn
asked. She looked out the window. "He's motioning,
Nick. You better stop.''

"Oh Lord! My muffler's probably belching black
smoke." Nick pulled over.

One of the Mounties got out and came to the car.
"Weren't you planning to go back to Kingston, Mr.
Barnaby?" he asked.

"Yes, as soon as I get my gas tank siphoned and refilled. Why? Isn't this the right route?"

"You're entering the ramp that heads east, not west."

"I see." He leveled an accusing look at Dawn. "My copilot misdirected me."

"If you're worried about your car, there *is* a service station a mile east of here. That might be your best bet. Then you can take the next exit off the Scenic and head back west."

"I'll do that. Thanks, Officer."

"Do you want an escort for the last mile?" The Mountie's tone made it clear that he didn't feel it was necessary.

"We should be all right. Thanks again."

The officer looked in the car window and saw the gun. "It might be a good idea to put that away," he suggested. Dawn hurriedly stuffed it into the glove compartment. "Good luck, Mr. Barnaby, ma'am." He saluted Dawn, and returned to his car.

Nick turned to Dawn and said, "Now it'll break down. Just watch it. We're going to be stranded on the highway. Oh, the joys of motoring. And you're not even wearing shorts."

"What's that got to do with it?" Dawn asked.

"To get a car to stop and help us. I thought you were an old movie freak. *It Happened One Night*— Claudette Colbert, Clark Gable."

"She didn't wear shorts. She wore a skirt. What I should have worn is nylons, so I could lift my skirt and fix my garter."

"I suppose you could lift your skirt and fix your knee," he suggested. "Adjust a Band-Aid or something."

"Yes, if I had a Band-Aid, which I don't. Stop worrying, Nick. The car sounds fine. It's just smoke."

"Where there's smoke, there's fire," he said fatalistically.

It was hard to enjoy the scenery, with Nick in such a morose mood. Dawn suspected he was talking about his car as a countermeasure against his worry about the diamonds. She soon spotted a service station sign and pointed it out to Nick.

"Thank God for that," he said, and pulled in.

He got out to speak to the attendant, and Dawn looked around. There was a coffee shop adjacent to the garage. After a few minutes Nick came over and said, "We're in luck. This is a full garage, not just a service station. The mechanic's going to siphon out the oil, refill the tank and run the car a few minutes to see if it's okay. It'll take a while, and he's checking the rear wheels of that pickup truck at the moment. Do you want to get out and stretch your legs?"

Dawn looked at the beat-up old red truck, which was carrying a load of two-by-fours. "I wouldn't mind a cup of coffee." The nerve-racking morning was taking its toll. "I'll wait inside while you hover over your car."

"You make me sound like a neurotic!" he exclaimed. "I'm not worried now. I'll go with you."

They went into the small, hot restaurant. The air was thick with the smell of bacon and coffee. There was a burly customer at the counter, talking to the cook cum waiter cum cashier. The customer's big shoulders were hunched over the counter. Dawn noticed that he had real strawberry-blond hair, the color she liked to imagine hers was. His conversation told them he was the driver of the pickup truck. "They'll be wondering what happened to that load of lumber," the man said, but he didn't seem worried.

Dawn looked around the shabby room. The floor was covered with chipped linoleum. On the walls hung calendars with pictures of women in bathing suits. She realized she was hungry after not eating her breakfast, but the thought of eating here didn't appeal to her.

"Let's sit by the window," she suggested. "At least the view will be good, whatever the coffee's like." The river sparkled below them. Far out in the channel, big steamships plied the waves, and closer to shore, local fishermen dangled their rods in the water.

The coffee was excellent. Over the first cup, they talked about their morning, and why Bloucher or his replacement hadn't shown up.

"Gloria will be wondering what's happened to us," Dawn said.

"I could call her at the hotel from here," Nick said. "She mentioned hiring a car. There's no reason for her to wait for us. She could rejoin the tour and keep an eye on Bloucher for us. I'd better give her a buzz."

He got change and went to the pay phone outside. Dawn waited, enjoying her coffee and pretending not to notice that the truck driver kept looking at her. Although the coffee was a stimulant, it had a calming effect on her nerves. Or maybe what she needed at this point was a stimulant.

Nick soon returned. "Great minds think alike," he said. "She was just checking out. She's going to try to meet up with the bus at Port Hope. I doubt if she'll make it, but if not, she'll go on to Toronto. She's a very plucky lady," he added admiringly.

Dawn tried not to be small-minded about that compliment, but it stung to hear Nick praise another woman. "Yes," she said. "The best of luck to her."

"How about another coffee? The mechanic was just starting on my car, so it'll be a while yet."

"Sure."

The counterman and the truck driver were deeply engrossed in conversation, so Nick went to get the pot himself to fill their cups. His back was to the door when a man came in. It wasn't the man's appearance that made Dawn suspicious. She hadn't seen Bloucher, and only knew that he was tall and thin, and that yesterday he had worn a white shirt. The tall, thin man at the door wore a blue shirt. No, it wasn't his looks that raised goose bumps on her arms. It was the way he looked at her, with a malicious smile of satisfaction.

She noticed he was carrying a newspaper in a peculiar way, draped over his hand—as if he was concealing something. A gun! She looked wildly to Nick. He was just coming back.

"The pot's empty," he said, "but there's a fresh one nearly ready." He noticed her frozen expression. "Dawn, what's the matter?" he exclaimed.

Her face was white, and her eyes stared as if she'd seen a ghost. He followed the direction of her look and saw Bloucher, smiling like a hyena. Nick recognized him instantly. In a few swift strides, Bloucher was at their table. He sat down, putting his hand, still covered by the newspaper, on the table. "Sit down," he said to Nick, in a menacing voice. Nick sat down.

"Yes, I *do* have a gun pointed at the young lady," he continued. He smiled, and used a polite tone to avoid rousing the suspicions of the other occupants. The truck driver merely glanced at him. "But there's no reason for anyone to get hurt. Just hand over the items, Miss Roberts, and we'll all be on our way."

Dawn's throat was dry, and her breath came in shallow gasps. A gun, pointed at her! "I don't have them," she said.

"Oh, come now. Your dear friend Mr. Hofstetter told me otherwise. He put them in your purse. Why would you have taken out that one container, and left everything else exactly as he described? Have you already given them to your friend?" he asked, turning to look at Nick. "They were missing from your purse yesterday. And while we're on the subject of your friend, let us all introduce ourselves."

Bloucher didn't know who he was! Nick thought rapidly. Was there any advantage in keeping his identity secret? No, that would concentrate Bloucher's attention on Dawn. Better to admit who he was. "Mr. Barnaby," he said.

"I suspected as much. Of the house of Verely, of course. I wasn't sure. Since you've been at pains to ingratiate yourself with Miss Roberts, I can only assume you have recovered your property, Mr. Barnaby?" His inflection made it a question.

Nick was desperate to find out where Werfel had hidden his diamonds, and decided to keep the discussion going as long as possible, hoping that Bloucher would reveal the truth. "A strange thing happened on our way to Kingston," Nick said. "Miss Roberts carelessly misplaced the—item that Mr. Werfel told you about."

Bloucher's shrewd, calculating eyes narrowed. "That's just ridiculous enough to be true," he said. "I can't think why else the two of you would still be together, traveling away from your tour."

"How did you find us?" Nick asked, to prolong the conversation. He hoped Bloucher was human enough to want to brag about his cleverness.

"I watched and waited." Bloucher smiled. "You didn't board the bus, nor did the third member of your party, that attractive blonde. No, you went to your car. And before long, the blonde followed you in another car. I assume the pair of broad shoulders with her belonged to a policeman. I prefer not to tangle with cops. I followed them at a discreet distance. When I saw them stop, I pulled in and waited. They didn't spot my car as they drove back. I waited for you to follow them, but you didn't, so I stepped on the gas and tailed you. I'd have been here sooner if I hadn't missed your turnoff, and had to double back. But enough about me," he said.

Every nerve in Dawn's body was stretched to the breaking point. Every rattle of Bloucher's newspaper was like a death threat. She wanted to scream aloud that she didn't have the diamonds and didn't know where they were. But fear held her silent. Nick directed a penetrating stare at her. He was trying to tell her something, but what? It might be best to say nothing. Maybe he was trying to trick Bloucher into revealing something.

"So, Mr. Barnaby," Bloucher said. "Shall we get on with it? The diamonds have been misplaced. We'll run over your itinerary and see if we can remember when this regrettable loss occurred. Since I assume you're on your way back to Rockwood Manor, where the tour stopped yesterday, they must have been left behind there."

Nick's mind rapidly considered this idea. Yes, that would give them some time. They'd all have to go back to Rockwood Manor. He'd try to find a chance to overpower Bloucher. If he could get to his car and get his gun.... He should have brought it in with him, but who would have thought Bloucher was following them? The man's next words threw Nick into uncertainty.

"The young lady will come along with me, just to make sure you don't get any funny ideas."

Dawn gulped and sat like a statue, paralyzed with fear. She had to go alone with Bloucher! And what would he say, what would he do when she admitted she had no idea where the diamonds were? The newspaper rattled ominously.

"No!" Nick said pugnaciously. His chin tilted up, and his lips firmed. "We all go together." Bloucher gave him a suspicious look. "My car's in trouble," Nick added. "That's why we're here. You must have seen the mechanic looking at it. The engine's heating up. It was smoking."

Bloucher took his decision. "Very well. We go in my car. You drive. The young lady sits in the back with me."

The waiter called across the room. "That coffee's ready now, Mac. You want some?"

Bloucher said, "Tell him no."

"Just the bill, thanks. We have to leave," Nick said.

"That'll be a buck fifty for two coffees. No charge for seconds," he added temptingly.

"Leave the money on the table," Bloucher said.

Nick felt that if he could just speak to the waiter, he might be able to give a message, or at least create a diversion. If he could get that bruiser of a truck driver to help him.... He pulled out his wallet and glanced inside. "I only have twenties," he said. "It'd look odd, leaving a tip that size."

Wanting to be helpful, Dawn opened her purse and took out her wallet. "I have a five," she said.

Bloucher reached in his pocket with his left hand and drew out two dollar bills. He threw them on the table, holding the newspaper at an awkward angle to hide the gun.

Dawn shoved her wallet back into her purse. It caught on something and she looked down. It was the big bottle of sunscreen cream Mr. McDougall had returned to her just before the bus left. It felt heavy in her hand. If she could manage to hit Bloucher a good crack on the head with it, it might not knock him out, but it would stun him at least, and give Nick a chance to hit him. Her fingers closed over the bottle. It fit in her palm neatly; it was just a little smaller than a baseball.

If only she could create a diversion to allow herself to get behind Bloucher and hit him. But she'd have to be fast. He was already pushing back his chair. The waiter and the truck driver glanced at them as they rose to leave. She turned her head slowly and gave the driver a big wink. He grinned, but he was ready to let it go at that. She had to increase his interest, make him think she was trying to pick him up, which wasn't easy when she was already with two men.

She remembered Miss Edmond's disgust at Gloria's stuffing a note in Nick's pocket. She could let the truck driver think she was giving him her phone number. She fingered her wallet, and pulled out one of her mother's catering cards. She lifted it and waved it at the driver. He eased off his stool and took a few steps toward them. He was built like a bull—wide, heavy-set and close to the ground. But she still didn't see any way of actually speaking to him, and she hadn't had time to write anything on the card.

In desperation, she gave him another smile, and dropped the card. Maybe he'd pick it up and use it as an excuse to start a conversation. Bloucher wasn't paying much attention to her, anyway. He obviously thought Nick was more likely to make trouble.

"Hey, you guys!" the waiter called. "That's a buck fifty. You pay here."

Bloucher turned toward him. "The money's on the table," he said. "Keep the change."

Nick was ransacking his mind, and tried a diversion of his own. "You should pay people for drinking that slop," he said. "It tasted like dishwater."

The waiter took exception to that. "Are you putting me on, Mac? I got the best coffee on this whole strip. Ask anybody. Ask Ed here." He nodded to the truck driver.

Nick gave Ed a disparaging look and said, "Ed doesn't look as if he could tell coffee from catsup."

"Come on," Bloucher urged, and waved his newspaper.

He was too late. Ed saw his chance to be a hero in front of the cute redhead and grabbed Nick by the shoulder. He spun him around and raised a fist the size of a ham hock.

Nick smiled apologetically and said, "Just kidding, Ed." He tried to convey a message with his eyes. He screwed up his face and kept looking at Bloucher.

"Come on," Bloucher repeated.

Ed was more interested in Dawn. He saw her beseeching gaze. "What the hell's going on here?" he demanded. "Are you all right with these kooks, lady?"

Bloucher's newspaper slipped, and the waiter shouted, "Cripes, he's got a gun!"

Bloucher uttered a few profanities and dropped the newspaper. He waved the gun in the general direction of Ed and Nick, with the waiter a few yards beyond them. The room was suddenly dead silent. Into the quiet he said, "You." He tossed his head toward Dawn. "Go get my car and bring it to the door." He held out the keys in his left hand. "And don't try anything if you know what's good for Barnaby."

She took the keys carefully, while he held the gun on Nick. At the doorway, she turned and surveyed the scene. The back of Bloucher's head was facing her, a clear, unimpeded target. Her fingers clenched around the heavy bottle of sunscreen. She could do it. Just pretend his shoulder was home base. Wind up, and let him have her curveball.

Nick watched mesmerized, as if seeing it all in slow motion. He didn't recognize the bottle in her hand at first, and thought she had somehow got hold of a ball. His first surge of joy was tempered when the bottle left her hand and flew in what looked like the wrong direction. It was veering off to the right. In midair, it changed direction and winged its way directly toward Bloucher's head.

It made a hollow thunk when it connected, and rolled off to a corner. Bloucher blinked once, and sank slowly to the floor, not knowing what had hit him. It was Ed who came pelting forward, laughing and congratulating her.

He pulled her into his arms. "That's quite an arm you got on you, lady. To say nothing of other parts," he added with an appreciative smile. "What the hell's going on here anyway? Did these guys kidnap you or something?"

"Just the one on the floor." She grinned and detached herself from Ed's arms to join Nick.

"Out like a light," Nick said. "Good work, Dawn. Let's tie him up before he comes to. Do you happen to have any handcuffs in that grab bag you carry?"

While Ed and the waiter exchanged excited comments, she rooted in the purse's depths and extracted a blue scarf. Nick rolled Bloucher over and tied his hands behind his back. The waiter was already on the phone, calling the police.

"What's going down?" Ed demanded.

"He belongs to a gang of diamond thieves," Dawn explained, pointing at Bloucher.

Ed gave her a skeptical look. "This is *Candid Camera*, right? Where's the camera?" He began tidying his hair and straightening his shirt.

"It's for real," she assured him.

"Go on, nothing ever happens here."

"It did today."

The waiter came forward. "I called the OPP," he said.

"Who?" Nick asked.

"The Ontario Provincial Police. This isn't a town. The OPP police the area. Just traffic usually."

"You'd better notify the Mounties, too," Dawn said. "Officer Hawthorn. He's at a hotel in Kingston." She gave him the name of the hotel, and the waiter, his head spinning, placed the call.

Once arrangements were under way, there was nothing to do but wait. "I guess there's no point in offering you coffee," the waiter said, still offended at Nick's slur.

"I was just trying to create a diversion," Nick explained. "The coffee's great, Mr.—I don't think I caught your name."

"Call me Steve," he said, and pumped Nick's hand. "Coffee, then?"

"Why not?"

The OPP were the first to arrive on the scene. A black and white car with a gold emblem pulled up, siren wailing, and a policeman got out. He looked impressive in his blue uniform, with his hand on his holster, ready to draw if necessary.

"Trouble, Steve?" he asked. "These guys trying to leave without paying, eh?"

"No, its *real* trouble," Steve said importantly. "We got a guy tied up in here."

The officer tried to look unconcerned, but his face turned pink. "What's the charge?"

"He stole some diamonds from this guy," Ed chimed in, pointing to Nick. He turned aside to Steve. "If this is *Candid Camera*, I hope you cleared it with the cops first."

"This ain't *Candid Camera*, Ed. Haven't you got a load of lumber to deliver?"

"I'm a witness," Ed objected. "A material witness," he added importantly.

When Bloucher regained consciousness, the officer helped him onto a chair and handcuffed him to it. Then he took a statement from Nick and Dawn. He was clearly happy to hear that the Mounties were on their way. "I'd better stick around to lend a hand," he decided, and sat down to enjoy a free cup of Steve's coffee.

It wasn't long before Hawthorn arrived with another officer. "So this is Bloucher," he said. Bloucher sat silent with his head down, and a sullen look on his face. "He'll talk when we get him booked. We'll need your testimony, folks," he said to Nick and Dawn. "I hope you're not in a hurry to get away."

Nick looked a question at Dawn. "You didn't really want to see that Blue Jays game, did you?" he asked apologetically.

"It'd be best if you could hang around Kingston for a few days," Hawthorn suggested. "You'll find plenty to do there. Swimming, boating, tourist stuff—Old Fort Henry."

"We never did see Old Fort Henry," Dawn said resignedly.

"I'd appreciate it if you'd come to my office as soon as possible," Hawthorn said, and gave them the directions. "I'll take Bloucher along with me. You got your diamonds, didn't you, Mr. Barnaby?"

Nick gave him a blank look. "No," he said, "but Bloucher knows where they are. I hope you can get it out of him."

"We will, eventually," Hawthorn said, and left.

"My car must be ready by now," Nick said.

Dawn and he took their leave of Ed and Steve and went back to the Jag. "Does it run all right?" Nick asked the mechanic.

"It'll be fine. You didn't drive far enough to do any real damage. You should never put oil in your gas tank though, sir. It's gas you use. That's why they call it a gas tank," he explained patiently.

"Thank you," Nick said, trying not to smile. "I'll remember that."

While he was signing the bill, Dawn decided to go back inside and thank Ed and Steve. Their leave-taking had been very confused, and she especially wanted to explain to Ed why she had winked at him.

"Ah, that's all right," he said with a blush. "I knew it couldn't be for real—a girl like you coming on to me."

She smiled. "I bet all the girls come on to you. Anyway thanks. And you, too, Steve. You were great."

"The paper's coming to take our pictures," Ed said proudly. It wasn't *Candid Camera*, but it was better than nothing.

"McQuaid'll be lucky if he gets his lumber this week," Steve said. "Oh, before you go, Miss Roberts. You might as well take your cream with you." He handed her the bottle that had rolled into the corner. "You've got a real neat curveball."

"Thanks." She slipped the cream in her purse and went back outside.

Nick had the car's top up that day, but the sun was so warm that she thought he might put it down. She'd applied some sunscreen earlier to protect herself. The little tube she'd bought at the hotel was stronger, so she decided to use it.

Nick was just putting his wallet in his pocket when she came out. "Just kissing Ed goodbye, were you?" he asked.

"That's right. What do you say we put the top down?"

"Good idea."

The racy sports car ate up the miles as they sped back to Kingston, discussing their adventure.

"I felt so helpless," Nick said. "And then to be rescued by a woman."

"Don't feel badly," she consoled him. "Ed's a lot bigger than you, and he didn't make any move on Bloucher."

"No, he was too busy making moves on you. Besides, he has an excuse. He didn't know what was going on."

"There wasn't much you could do, with that gun pointing at you. That was a good try, insulting Steve's coffee. That's what really started the rumble."

Her efforts at reassurance only made him feel worse. "You don't have to patronize me. I was rescued by a woman. A small woman, who probably doesn't even weigh a hundred pounds."

"A hundred and five, actually. I'm compact. Now if I could only rescue your diamonds, I could go to Toronto and see the Blue Jays," she said. "Werfel told Bloucher he put them in my purse."

"Did you discard anything at Rockwood Manor? Some cosmetics or something that you didn't like? That's obviously what Bloucher thought."

Dawn carefully ran over that visit to Rockwood. "No, nothing. I brought everything on to Kingston with me. My cosmetics bag and my sunscreen...." Her sunscreen? She frowned, remembering that she had been separated from it for a while. She had left it behind on the table just before Bloucher snatched her bag and searched it. A quiver of excitement tingled along her fingers. "You examined everything. I wonder...." She took out the big bottle of sunscreen.

"I hope you're not planning to wing that at *me*," Nick said.

"Did you search this when you checked out my purse?" she asked. "In Gananoque, I mean. Gloria said you'd looked through my bag."

"I dabbled a finger in it. Why?"

"Because this is the only thing Bloucher didn't examine." She unscrewed the cap and carefully stuck her index finger deep into the cream. She felt something hard against her finger. She pushed it to the side and lifted it out. It looked like a sharp-edged pebble. Her heart pounded. "Nick, I think you'd better stop the car," she said quietly.

"We're nearly there."

"Stop the car," she repeated.

"You're not going to be sick!" Nick exclaimed. He pulled over to the shoulder.

She rubbed the pebble on the palm of her hand to remove the cream and stared at a brilliant-cut diamond about the size of a cherry pit. Nick looked down and saw it catching the slanting rays of the sun and reflecting prisms on the leather upholstery of the dashboard. "Good God!" he said, and reached for it.

Chapter Ten

Dawn plunged her finger in again, and lifted out a pear-cut stone. "There are more. I can feel them," she exclaimed excitedly.

Nick cradled the gem in the palm of his hand. "It's incredible!" he whispered, staring at it. "They were here all the time. I even opened that cream pot. It looked so gooey I just stuck my finger in. I didn't think Werfel would have time to get to the jar."

"He was holding some of my things while I looked for my ID at the border," Dawn said. "That must be when he did it."

"The diamonds probably sank to the bottom as you moved around." They were both fishing in the cream now, taking turns and lifting out stones.

"How many altogether?" she asked.

"Thirty. We don't have to bother fishing them all out. We can do that at the hotel." Nick shoved the diamonds he was holding back into the pot and Dawn did the same. She rearranged the cream smoothly on top and put on the lid.

He turned to her, his eyes glowing, his whole face radiant with joy. "Did I happen to mention I love you, Dawn Roberts?" he asked, and kissed her. It was a loud, playful smack on the cheek.

Dawn was sure it was just gratitude and relief talking, and damped down her own pleasure. "I bet you say that to all your detective friends," she answered carelessly.

"No, only to you. I'm going to buy you a diamond as big as the Ritz."

"Great, I'll turn it into a condo. I sure couldn't wear it around my neck."

"That's hyperbole, Dawn. An intended exaggeration." He looked deep into her eyes and added, "And around your neck isn't where I meant you to wear it."

Before she quite realized what he was talking about, he put the car in gear and drove back onto the highway. "It isn't a good idea for us to carry these with us," he said.

"I know what you mean. I feel as if I'm carrying a bomb in my purse," she replied nervously.

"I'll put them in a safety deposit box in Kingston till I can arrange to have them taken to New York."

"I wonder how long we'll have to stick around Kingston."

"Just long enough to give our deposition. Bloucher will be extradited to the States for trial." Nick laughed again. He was in that kind of mood, giddy with happiness.

When the excitement of the find began to wear off, Dawn realized she was actually more depressed than anything else. Her adventure was over. She couldn't regret that it had happened. It had turned her little holiday into a once-in-a-lifetime romantic intrigue. She'd never forget it—that was exactly the trouble. Life would seem so dreary after this taste of excitement. Other men would seem so dull after Nick.

"There's old Henry again," Nick said, as they drove past the fort. "Let's give him a wave. This is probably as close as we'll get to meeting him."

"You mentioned we might go there this afternoon," Dawn reminded him.

"We could, if there's time," he agreed. "I'll be pretty busy. As well as giving Hawthorn a statement, I'll have to make arrangements to have the diamonds delivered home. That may take some doing, finding a bonded courier in a small city. And of course I'll have to talk to Gloria, to let her know we—*you*—found the diamonds. She'll probably hop the first train or plane back to Kingston."

There goes our evening, Dawn thought to herself. She knew she had outdone Gloria in the case. She had found the diamonds, and she had rescued them from Bloucher, so there was no reason to feel insecure about glamorous Gloria. Except that finding the diamonds didn't make her any taller, or more beautiful, or sophisticated. And if it made Nick say he loved her, that was only temporary. Hyperbole, like promising her a diamond as big as the Ritz.

"We'll all go out and paint the town red," Nick said. "We'll invite Hawthorn, too." That would give Gloria an escort, and allow him some time with Dawn. "I bet the cops don't get included in most of their clients' celebrations. Besides, he's local. He'll know the best places to go. It'll be your night, Dawn. You're the heroine."

It sounded like being queen for a day, but she didn't want to spoil Nick's pleasure, and tried to simulate enthusiasm. Maybe Gloria and Hawthorn would hit it off. She had called him John, after all. She didn't have to be nice to him in the way of business, so maybe she found him attractive. Dawn realized that while her mind was wondering, Nick had been chattering on enthusiastically, and she shook herself back to attention.

"Naturally Verely will pay all your expenses," he was saying. "We'll hire you a suite for as long as you have to stay in town. Live it up. You've earned it. Champagne for breakfast, the works."

They were driving into the city now. "Do you have any objection to going back to the hotel we were at before?" he asked. "The location was good, and we'll ask for better rooms than the tour provided."

"That's fine," she said. "There was nothing wrong with my old room. I don't need a suite, and I don't particularly want champagne for breakfast, either."

He gave her an intimate smile that wrenched at her insides. "You can take the girl out of the kitchen, but you can't take the kitchen out of the girl, huh? Are you sure you wouldn't be happier at the Y?"

"I have nothing against it," she said, annoyed at his patronizing attitude, even if he was joking.

"I do. It's that business of separate YWs and YMs that puts me off."

Nick drove under the covered entrance to the hotel and opened the car door for Dawn. "You have our cream safe?" he asked in a stage whisper.

She patted her bag. "Right here."

"Good, I'll get the luggage."

They went to the desk and Nick arranged for their rooms. He acted as porter again, carrying the bags. When he unlocked her door, she stepped in and felt lost in what looked like a movie star's boudoir. Across an expanse of white carpet, a canopied bed loomed. Swaths of gauzy chiffon lent a cloudlike look to the wall of windows. The furnishings were white French provincial.

Nick bowed like a butler. "There's a sitting room through here for *madame*'s use."

Dawn was determined not to show how impressed she was. "Gee, there's a chair by the vanity. Do I need a whole room, just to sit?"

"It comes complete with stereo, TV, bar, etcetera. Want a soft drink?" he offered in a less elevated tone.

"That'd be fine."

Nick went into the sitting room and came back with two cans. "We have glasses and ice," he said, "but I get the impression you're not in the mood for the finer things of life."

Dawn determined to be less touchy. "Sure I am. Let's fish out the diamonds and look at them."

"I thought you'd never ask. I'd better get something to wipe them off."

He brought a towel from the bathroom and Dawn took out the jar of cream. "Let's empty the cream on something, and make sure we get out all the stones," she suggested.

"Right, but first let's put the chain on the door, just in case."

They used a tray that held glasses for the job. Dawn scooped out the cream. Embedded in it like currants in dough were the diamonds. She and Nick fished them out and wiped them off. They came in various sizes and cuts. A rectangular emerald-cut stone was the largest, but not the prettiest. When they were all cleaned off, Nick counted them.

"Yup, they're all here. Thirty of them." In this corner away from the window, they glimmered, but they didn't show to best advantage.

To Dawn, they looked like a little pile of chipped glass. "It's amazing to think these are worth three million dollars," she said. "I wouldn't give a week's wages for any of them."

Nick looked offended. "They look better when they're mounted. I think this one would be good for you," he said, and took a brilliant-cut stone of about five carats from the little heap. "I like a Tiffany setting myself. It's old-fashioned, but it would suit you." He envisaged it matched with a very plain traditional gold wedding band.

She looked at him, startled. "Suit me? I don't want a diamond ring. I don't even like them much. You don't have to give me a reward," she said. "Let's call Hawthorn, and find your courier, so we can get out of here."

Nick examined her with a penetrating stare. She didn't want a diamond ring. All she wanted was to get out of here. Was she saying she had no intention of marrying him? He saw the impatient, rather cross expression she wore, and knew this wasn't the time to press her.

"Right," he said, and picked up the phone.

Dawn wandered around the rooms while Nick arranged the meeting with the Mountie. She felt out of place, almost lost in the vast opulence of the suite. It was overkill, like that big square diamond that Nick said was worth half a million dollars. People were crazy to waste their money on things like that. Nick was probably paying two or three hundred dollars a day for these rooms.

She looked at the brocade drapes at the window, and through the sheer curtains to the water and busy wharf below. It was awfully nice, though. Over her shoulder, she looked back into the bedroom, where the canopied bed stood out against a wall covered by pale, flowered paper. There was a brass antique lamp next to the bed, so pretty it looked like sculpture. Then she turned and looked at Nick.

His dark head was bent down. He was fingering his diamonds as he talked to Hawthorn on the phone. He looked at home in this setting. Maybe that was why she didn't like the place. It was a reminder of the differences in their backgrounds. This setting was typical of Nick's life; for her it was a unique brush with glamour. She couldn't let herself enjoy it. It would make it that much harder when she had to return to reality.

Nick hung up the phone and went into the sitting room. "Not enjoying the chaise longue, I see." He grinned. "Since you're on your feet, you won't mind going down to headquarters, and getting it over with?"

"Aren't you going to call Gloria?" she asked.

"She wouldn't have reached Toronto yet. That can wait."

"Let's go, then."

"You don't just 'go,' when you're carrying diamonds," he explained. "Hawthorn is coming to pick us up, with an armed officer. He says he'll need to hold the evidence for a few days. The RCMP are going to arrange delivery to New York afterward, which is a vast relief to me, I can tell you. He's coming right down."

"You might as well take your luggage to your room," she said. "I want to freshen up."

Nick scooped the diamonds into his handkerchief and knotted it. "I'll be back in a flash," he said. Before he left, he kissed his finger and put it on her lips. They felt soft and warm. "How can I ever make it up to you, Dawn?" He examined her, thinking that even her name was lovely. Dawn sounded fresh and young and dewy, and full of promise.

She moved her head, dislodging his finger. "It wasn't your fault that Werfel chose me."

His finger slid down to her chin, and he pinched it. "I'm glad he did. If he hadn't, we never would have met."

"No, I doubt if we'd have met in Scranton, and I don't get to Europe very often," she said, trying not to sound bitter.

"Do you dislike that, too? I know you have a low opinion of diamonds." His fingers stroked her jaw.

"I only object to the price of travel."

His lips lifted in a smile. "It's not that expensive," he said softly. "You know the old saying, two can travel as cheaply as one."

"That's two can live as cheaply as one, isn't it?"

"Even better. Think about it." He patted her cheek and left.

Dawn thought about it. What was he suggesting? Money was no object to Nick Barnaby. He had already suggested a trip to Paris. What was he hinting at now? A longer liaison? If he thought she was interested in cohabiting, he was out of his mind. But she admitted she was flattered that the idea had occurred to him, that he liked her enough to even think of it. It was probably just euphoria at having his precious diamonds back.

Nearly an hour passed before Nick and Hawthorn came to Dawn's room. She hadn't thought it would take so long. In a little city like this, the RCMP headquarters couldn't be that far away. In the interval, she washed her face and hands and brushed her hair. When that was done, she cleaned up the cream from the tray and washed it. After she had replaced the glasses on the tray, she realized that room service would have cleared away the mess. She wasn't used to having servants look after her. With time to spare, she got out the itinerary of the Pennypinchers' tour, and tried to calculate how soon she could rejoin it. But her heart was no longer in it. Miss Edmonds and the McDougalls promised to be dull company after Nick.

Her door was locked, and when the tap finally came, she peered out the peephole to make sure it was Nick and Hawthorn before opening it. The officer with Hawthorn stayed outside the door, guarding it. Nick and Hawthorn were both in a jubilant mood.

"Once Bloucher heard you'd found the diamonds, he admitted everything," Hawthorn said. "We've been in touch with New York. They'll be sending some men up to take him home. I can take your deposition here and let you folks get on with your holiday."

Nick said to Dawn, "The sitting room will be useful after all."

Hawthorn wrote swiftly as Nick outlined the affair from the beginning, starting with his mother's purchase of the diamonds in London. Hawthorn seemed interested in all the details, perhaps thinking they might prove useful in another case. "And Miss Roberts was carrying around three million dollars' worth of diamonds, without knowing it,'' he said, shaking his head.

"Leaving them sitting unguarded at poolside tables, and in my room,'' she added. "And heaven only knows where else Mrs. McDougall kept them. We're lucky her girls didn't decide to play with the cream.''

"Your guardian angel must have been at work.'' Hawthorn smiled. "If they'd been in your purse when Bloucher attacked you, he'd have gotten away with them. I'll need an account of his attack on you as well, Miss Roberts.''

Dawn retold that story, and Nick identified Bloucher as her attacker. The whole deposition only took half an hour. Hawthorn signed a receipt for the diamonds, and promised Nick he'd have them back soon. "Whether the American officials release them immediately or not, I wouldn't know,'' he added.

Nick rubbed his hands and gave a mock-evil grin. "We have ways of making them obey.''

Hawthorn nodded. "I don't imagine you'll have any trouble. I'll be off now. It was nice meeting you, folks. Good luck.'' He shook their hands and left.

"Didn't you ask him out with us tonight?'' Dawn asked, when they were alone.

"I put out a feeler. He's married, so I didn't mention painting the town red.''

"Oh, I see.'' So it would be the three of them.

Nick looked at his watch. "Meanwhile, it's twelve-thirty, and time we had lunch. Shall we go? John suggested an outdoor café, just a couple of blocks away. We could walk.''

"Fine.''

They went downstairs. Frank Francis was back on duty, and accosted them. "I saw the Mounties going upstairs. What's new on the case?"

Nick told him briefly.

"I'm glad you got them back. And this little lady is the heroine of the day," Frank said, looking Dawn up and down and shaking his head. "It just goes to show you."

"I wonder what he meant by that?" Dawn said as they went out into the sunlight. The sky was so blue, and the day so lovely that she felt her spirits rise spontaneously. She wouldn't spoil the rest of this adventure with regrets that it couldn't last forever. It had been a great holiday, and she'd just try to think of it as a brief interval in her life.

Nick said, "I guess he meant you can't judge a book by its cover, or a lady by her size. Something like that. You certainly fooled me."

"What do you mean?"

"Here I thought you were just another pretty face, and you were packing a lethal curveball all the time. I'll have to remember that." He stopped and turned to face her. "Would you conk me on the head if you caught me running away from you, Dawn?"

"That'd depend on why you were running. If you'd stolen my wallet, I probably would."

He took her hand and resumed walking. "It's not your wallet I'm after," he said.

They were at a crossing, and with heavy traffic to watch for, Dawn had to wait to follow up that intriguing statement. When they were safely on the other side of the street, she said, "I didn't think it was. My two hundred dollars worth of mad money wouldn't be of much interest to an old tycoon like you."

"Old?" he asked swiftly. "I haven't started to lose my hair yet. I'm only thirty-one."

Since his age seemed to bother him, Dawn decided to goad him a little. "That sounds pretty ancient to me. I'll slow down. I don't want to tire you out."

"Don't patronize me, young lady. I'll have you know I'm in perfect shape."

She looked him up and down in a dispassionate way. "You're in pretty good shape. Arnold Schwarzenegger is in perfect shape."

"He's muscle-bound. I am in perfect shape. I work out, jog, play racquetball. And watch TV, eat potato chips, read a lot," he admitted ruefully.

"Watch TV?" Dawn asked, amazed that such a mundane activity had crept into his agenda.

"What do you think I do, alone in some city where the only people I know are dull businessmen?"

"I thought you'd go out with women."

He gave a heavy frown. "Would I really be having such a hard time getting you, if I had all that vast cosmopolitan experience?"

"Getting me to what?" she asked with a suspicious eye.

"Why, to like diamonds, of course," he parried, grinning wickedly. "That sign up ahead—is it the Courtyard Café? Yes, and look at the crowd. I hope we don't have to wait."

"Slip them ten bucks."

"The voice of experience?" he asked archly.

"Yes, experience of watching TV. Of course I'm not sure it's a ten. Five might be enough."

"Twenty is more like it."

The early arrivals were leaving, and they didn't have to wait for a table. The café was surrounded by a link fence, and planted with bushes and flowers to add beauty. Colorful sun umbrellas gave the customers some privacy.

"This is downright civilized," Nick said, looking around. "You'd think we were at a sidewalk café in Paris."

"Except they don't have a TV," she said with a knowing look.

Nick moved his chair closer to hers. "Sometimes I get lucky, and have a real, live partner to eat with."

Dawn picked up the menu and studied it, to avoid continuing this little game of flirtation. "I'm going to have the fruit plate with cottage cheese. Oh look, Nick!" she added. "They have shrimp puffs as an appetizer. I have to try them, and see if they're as good as Mom's."

"I'll have the steak—and wine, to celebrate?"

"It doesn't go with fruit salad, does it?" she asked uncertainly.

"Champagne goes with anything. Let me order some."

"I'm not your keeper. Order whatever you want."

"But you'll join me?"

"Sure."

Nick gave the order. The wine came in an ice-filled bucket that stood beside their table. Diners at other tables looked at them and smiled when the waiter popped the cork. He poured a small quantity into one glass for Nick to test.

"May I wish the new couple every happiness," the waiter said, as he filled their glasses.

"We're not married!" Dawn exclaimed.

The waiter lifted his eyebrows in surprise. "My mistake," he said. "Usually when a young couple orders champagne, they are on their honeymoon."

The eyes of a few of the watchers widened in surprise at Dawn's reaction. One woman gave a high laugh. Dawn looked at Nick in vexation. "Did you hear that?" she said in a low voice. His teasing look annoyed her. "We're just celebrating!" she said loudly, aiming her voice at the next table.

Nick gave an embarrassed smile at the woman. He was rather annoyed at Dawn's loud protest. "I'm sure we don't have to apologize for ordering champagne," he said. Dawn felt gauche, as if she'd fractured some rule of dining etiquette.

"*Bon appetit*," the waiter said, and left.

The arrival of the shrimp puffs was a welcome diversion. "These are delicious," Dawn said. "Try one, Nick. They taste just like Mom's. I bet they use a little cornstarch in the batter, too, to make it so crisp."

Nick took one and nibbled the batter. "Nice," he said, and set it aside.

Dawn took his reaction as a personal insult. "What's the matter? Isn't shrimp *recherché* enough for you? You'd rather have truffles, I suppose."

He lifted his brows in surprise. "*Recherché*? My, my, aren't we bilingual."

She gave him a bellicose look. First he spurned the appetizer she had chosen, now he was criticizing her vocabulary. Who did he think he was anyway? "I've been studying French. There's no law against it, is there?"

"I doubt if they'll arrest you in Canada, in any case. It's one of their official languages. Why are you studying French?"

"For when I can afford to go to Paris, of course. Why do you think?" she snapped.

"I think we're arguing, but I can't quite figure out why. Is it the champagne? Surely the recovery of three million dollars' worth of property justifies one small extravagance."

"Your whole life is an extravagance!" Dawn said, blurting out the truth in the heat of the moment. "Renting that elaborate suite for me. I don't need all that room. You're just showing off. Your car, your trips to Europe...."

Nick saw all his efforts to impress her going up in smoke. Fear of losing her made him speak sharply. "It's business that takes me to Europe, not pleasure. All that travel is a pain in the neck, if you want the truth. You know how much my car means to me. You complained enough that I was worried about it. I don't buy toys like that every day, you know. And as to your suite, I was trying to impress you. Is it a crime for a guy to try to impress the woman he loves?"

Loves! The word exploded like a bomb between them. Dawn sat, trying to keep her jaw from dropping. She couldn't think of anything to say. It seemed unreal, that the worldly, sophisticated, outrageously handsome man beside her had just said he loved her.

"You made it pretty clear you weren't impressed by diamonds," he added.

Dawn gulped, and tried to undo the harm of her outburst. "I just don't think they're the prettiest gemstone," she said in a small, apologetic voice.

"And I hate shrimp," he said, quick to follow up her effort at reconciliation. "It's nothing personal. I'm sure you make great shrimp puffs, but I just don't like shrimp. I'm not crazy about truffles, if it comes to that, and besides, they're too expensive."

Dawn felt her lower lip trembling. She held it between her teeth a moment. "I've never tasted truffles," she said. Why were they babbling about shrimp and truffles, when Nick had just said he loved her? "The champagne is lovely," she said as a peace offering.

"I don't drink champagne for lunch every day, either," he assured her.

"I know," she said quickly. "Today you're celebrating recovering your diamonds."

Nick took her hand in his and squeezed till her fingers ached. In his eyes she read hope, and concern, and love. It was such a concentrated, penetrating look she could almost feel it. A warm glow spread through her, as if she were lying in the sun, receiving its life-giving heat.

"I was hoping we'd be celebrating more than that, Dawn," he said softly.

Dawn sat still, waiting. "Oh," she said with a small, encouraging smile.

The woman who had laughed was watching them. Nick stood up and adjusted the umbrella to give them total privacy.

"What are doing?" Dawn asked. But she had a pretty good idea what he was up to, and heartily approved.

He pulled her up from her chair, into his arms. "I'm trying to propose, darling. I don't want to lose you, Dawn. You're the best thing that ever happened to me. It crept up on me slowly at first. We're not as different as you think."

"We're miles apart," she said, but in a dreamy way.

"Not really. We just do different jobs, that happen to occur in different places. Mine takes me abroad, but I don't live there. I live an ordinary life. I'd like to live it with you. I can learn to love baseball."

Dawn gave an ecstatic sigh. "I guess I could learn to live with diamonds," she said.

"You can pick your own engagement ring, as long as I get to choose the groom—me."

His lips found hers and delivered a dizzying kiss. She didn't know how it had happened. She'd thought her romantic holiday was ending, but now she felt it was just the beginning of a lifelong romance. It was an irate voice from behind the umbrella that brought them back down to earth.

"If they're not married, they *should* be is all I can say!" a woman's querulous voice exclaimed. "Really! Right in public!" She sounded like Mrs. McDougall.

Nick lifted his head and gazed into the green dazzle of Dawn's eyes. An emerald, of course! What else would suit her as well? Cold, hard diamonds weren't right for her. "She's right, you know." He smiled. "We really should be married as soon as possible. What do you say we cut the tour short, and go home to make the arrangements?"

"Oh gosh, I—I guess I should phone Mom," Dawn said. "And you'll have to phone Gloria. But don't we have to stay till Hawthorn—"

"We're finished with Hawthorn. Gloria called while I was in my room before he came. She's not coming back. We could leave right now—right after lunch, and be in Scranton before dark. What do you say?"

"I wonder what Miss Edmonds will think! She warned me about you."

"Someone should have warned me."

Dawn looked uncertain. "Are you sorry you fell in love with me, Nick?" she asked. "I know I won't fit into your world at first." She knew by his expression that he had no doubts. "Mind you, I think I could get used to traveling first-class," she added.

"I'm delighted. *Warn* was the wrong word. You're a diamond of the first water— Uh-oh. Wrong stone. You're a home run, Dawn."

She lifted her glass. "Here's looking at us, kid."

Nick took his glass. "I'll drink to that," he said.

They touched glasses, and drank champagne in the sunlight.

* * * * *

Silhouette Romance®

LONG, TALL TEXANS

Diana Palmer brings you the second Award of Excellence title

SUTTON'S WAY

In Diana Palmer's bestselling Long, Tall Texans trilogy, you had a mesmerizing glimpse of Quinn Sutton—a mean, lean Wyoming wildcat of a man, with a disposition to match.

Now, in September, Quinn's back with a story of his own. Set in the Wyoming wilderness, he learns a few things about women from snowbound beauty Amanda Callaway—and a lot more about love.

He's a Texan at heart . . . who soon has a Wyoming wedding in mind!

The Award of Excellence is given to one specially selected title per month. Spend September discovering *Sutton's Way* #670 . . . only in Silhouette Romance.

RS670-1R

Silhouette Intimate Moments®

AWARD OF EXCELLENCE

NORA ROBERTS
brings you the first
Award of Excellence title
Gabriel's Angel
coming in August from
Silhouette Intimate Moments

They were on a collision course with love....

*Laura Malone was alone, scared—and pregnant. She was running
for the sake of her child. Gabriel Bradley had his own problems.
He had neither the need nor the inclination to get involved in
someone else's.*

*But Laura was like no other woman . . . and she needed him. Soon
Gabe was willing to risk all for the heaven of her arms.*

The Award of Excellence is given to one specially selected title per
month. Look for the second Award of Excellence title, coming out in
September from Silhouette Romance—**SUTTON'S WAY
by Diana Palmer**

Im 300-1

You'll flip . . . your pages won't!
Read paperbacks *hands-free* with

Book Mate·I

The perfect "mate" for all your romance paperbacks
Traveling • Vacationing • At Work • In Bed • Studying
• Cooking • Eating

Perfect size for
all standard
paperbacks,
this wonderful
invention
makes reading
a pure pleasure!
Ingenious
design holds
paperback
books OPEN
and FLAT so
even wind can't
ruffle pages –
leaves your
hands free to do
other things.
Reinforced,
wipe-clean vinyl-
covered holder flexes to let you
turn pages without undoing the
strap . . . supports paperbacks so
well, they have the strength of
hardcovers!

Pages turn WITHOUT
opening the strap

SEE-THROUGH STRAP

Reinforced back stays flat

Built in bookmark

BOOK MARK

BACK COVER
HOLDING STRIP

10 x 7¼ opened
Snaps closed for easy carrying too

Available now Send your name, address, and zip code, along with a check or
money order for just $5.95 + 75¢ for postage & handling (for a total of $6.70)
payable to Reader Service to

Reader Service
Bookmate Offer
901 Fuhrmann Blvd.
P.O. Box 1396
Buffalo, N.Y 14269-1396

Offer not available in Canada
* New York and Iowa residents add appropriate sales tax

BM-G

Silhouette Special Edition®

presents

★ LOVE AND GLORY ★

from
Lindsay McKenna

Introducing a gripping new series celebrating our men—and women—in uniform. Meet the Trayherns, a military family as proud and colorful as the American flag, a family fighting the shadow of dishonor, a family determined to triumph—with **LOVE AND GLORY!**

June: A QUESTION OF HONOR (SE #529) leads the fast-paced excitement. When Coast Guard officer Noah Trayhern offers Kit Anderson a safe house, he unwittingly endangers his own guarded emotions.

July: NO SURRENDER (SE #535) Navy pilot Alyssa Trayhern's assignment with arrogant jet jockey Clay Cantrell threatens her career—and her heart—with a crash landing!

August: RETURN OF A HERO (SE #541) Strike up the band to welcome home a man whose top-secret reappearance will make headline news . . . with a delicate, daring woman by his side.

Silhouette Romance®

JOIN TOP-SELLING AUTHOR *EMILIE RICHARDS* FOR A SPECIAL ANNIVERSARY

Only in September, and only in Silhouette Romance, we are bringing you Emilie's twentieth Silhouette novel, *Island Glory* (SR #675).

Island Glory brings back Glory Kalia, who made her first—and very memorable—appearance in *Aloha Always* (SR #520). Now she's here with a story—and a hero—of her own. Thrill to warm tropical nights with Glory and Jared Farrell, a man who doesn't want to give any woman his heart but quickly learns that, with Glory, he has no choice.

Join Silhouette Romance for September and experience a taste of *Island Glory*.